Hjalmar Hjorth Boyesen

Against heavy Odds

A Tale of Norse heroism

Hjalmar Hjorth Boyesen

Against heavy Odds
A Tale of Norse heroism

ISBN/EAN: 9783337072988

Printed in Europe, USA, Canada, Australia, Japan

Cover: Foto ©Andreas Hilbeck / pixelio.de

More available books at **www.hansebooks.com**

AGAINST HEAVY ODDS

A Tale of Norse Heroism

BY

HJALMAR HJORTH BOYESEN

AUTHOR OF "THE MODERN VIKINGS" "IDYLS OF NORWAY"
"GUNNAR" ETC.

ILLUSTRATED BY W. L. TAYLOR

NEW YORK
CHARLES SCRIBNER'S SONS
1890

UNIVERSITY PRESS:
JOHN WILSON AND SON, CAMBRIDGE.

CONTENTS.

———◆———

LIST OF ILLUSTRATIONS.

AGAINST HEAVY ODDS.

CHAPTER I.

"THE 'PETREL' HAS COME!"

CONSUL PREBENSEN'S barque, the "Petrel,"
was making for the harbor. The shot she
had fired for a pilot had given such a tremendous resonance in the frosty autumn air
that it had been heard in town; and now
all the population, both old and young, were
thronging down on the piers to give her a
right royal welcome.

For the prosperity of Vardöe was largely
bound up in the "Petrel." There was
scarcely a man, woman, or child outside of
the Lappish suburb who had not a relative
on board Consul Prebensen's barque. Some
had fathers, some brothers, some sweethearts,
and now they were to see them after an
absence of five months.

There had been much anxiety expressed
of late for the " Petrel; " and as the weeks
dragged themselves along in their slow mo-
notony up there within the Arctic Circle,
the anxiety had deepened into dread, and
the dread into certainty, that something had
happened to the ship.

Most likely she was only ice-bound, and
would drift southward when the ice broke up
in the spring; but in the mean while what
was to become of the wives and children at
home who had nothing to live on during
the long winter but the wages of the sailors?
Starvation stared them in the face; that
was the long and short of it.

But why consider what might have been,
now that the barque is in sight? There her
main-mast is seen looming up beyond the
island. Look how neatly her white top-sail
catches the breeze! And now the whole
beautiful " Petrel" is rounding the headland,
and a tremendous cheer greets her from the
pier.

Two small cannon, at a signal from the
consul, begin to bang away, and manage to

make an awful racket. The "Petrel" re-
sponds as gallantly as if she were a man-of-
war. As the red flash preceding the report
leaps out over the water, the girls on the pier
put their fingers in their ears and scream, and
the boys jeer at them and yell with delight.

"The 'Petrel' has come! the 'Petrel' has
come!" was the message that ran from house
to house like fire in withered grass; and if
anybody had doubted that the "Petrel" had
really come, those five or six cannon-shots
would have put an end to his doubts, for it
is not every day that people up there under
the North Pole can afford to fire cannon, and
Consul Prebensen, rich as he was, was not a
man to waste his powder.

Every man's pulses bounded, and every
woman's heart leaped in her breast, when
that salute was heard, and in five minutes
more the town was as if deserted. The mer-
chants locked their stores, putting the keys
in their pockets, and gave their clerks a
holiday; the smith and the carpenter pushed
away their tools, and with their aprons on,
hurried to the beach; and the servant-girls,

with disordered hair, joyously excited faces,
and sleeves rolled up to their elbows, climbed
upon bowlders and rocks, and stood shading
their eyes against the sun as they gazed at
the " Petrel."

It was said afterward that there were but
four persons of sound body and mind left
in Vardöe that morning, and they were Consul Prebensen's four clerks; for the consul
prided himself on his business principles.
He kept strict discipline in his store, and he
was not fond of holidays.

The " Petrel," after having fired her salute,
made two graceful tacks up the sound, and
it was lovely to see her luff round, with her
bright canvas all outspread, careening slightly
now to starboard, now to port, according as
she tacked. What enthusiasm she aroused
in the heart of every boy who stood there
on the pier yelling himself hoarse in her
honor !

One boy there was, however, in that crowd
who was not at all joyous. In him the return
of the ship awakened anything but happy
memories. Ingomar Vang remembered a

time when the "Petrel" had been in other
hands than those of Consul Prebensen. He
remembered bitterly the day when she came
from Grimstad, where she had been built,
with all her canvas swelling just as now, and
all the people for a month after talked of
nothing but Mr. Vang's beautiful barque.

Ingomar's father, who was of a mechanical
turn, had designed her, and it was for his
account and under his supervision that she
was put on the stocks and pushed forward
to completion.

Prebensen was then nothing but a clerk in
Mr. Vang's store, and not half so high and
mighty as he was now. The consul, who
now was the big man of the town, would not
have thanked any one who should have dared
to remind him how poor and forlorn he was
twenty-two years ago, when he presented
himself in Mr. Vang's office to apply for
work.

He had been an efficient clerk, there was
no doubt of that, and had gradually risen
by means of little ventures of his own, which
he had made on the sly, until he was able

to establish himself on his own account as Mr. Vang's rival. He prudently began in a small way in a little back street, where a shop could be had for next to nothing.

Mr. Vang was so far from suspecting a rival in his former clerk that he lent him more than once a helping hand when a tightness of the money-market or other causes threatened to ruin him. Kind-hearted and unsuspicious as Mr. Vang was, it took him a good while to discover that Prebensen was systematically and with malice afore-thought stealing his customers from him, and availing himself of the connections which he had made while in Vang's office to injure his credit and rise upon his shoulders.

The upright and honorable merchant had to have a good many proofs forced upon him before he could accept such a conclusion ; but Prebensen, as soon as he felt himself toler-ably firm in the saddle, did not care to keep him in uncertainty.

He captured the Lapp trade, which had contributed fully one half of Mr. Vang's income, right under the very nose of his former chief. He did it by all sorts of low arts to which a gentleman like Mr. Vang could not condescend. He established a brandy-shop in connection with his business, and succeeded in making it so attractive to the mountain Lapps who came to town to make purchases that they usually left pretty much all the earnings of the year in Prebensen's coffers.

He studied their superstitions in order to make money out of their credulity; he fraternized with them, and pretended to get tipsy with them, in order to pull his net the more surely over them; while they regarded him as a harmless, jolly young fellow.

To chronicle all the arts by which Mr. Prebensen had risen to his present eminence would make a considerable story in itself. Suffice it to say that he had not been scrupulous in his choice of means.

Having secured the Lapp trade, he began to throw out his toils in other directions. The house of Vang, though greatly hampered by its want of resources, had yet a considerable income from its ships that sailed

every spring on sealing and whaling expeditions into the Arctic Ocean; but to equip
these expeditions required capital, and two
bad fishing seasons, which compelled the
house to extend its credit and cut off its
supply of cash, brought Prebensen his
opportunity.

For Prebensen **rarely** gave credit, except
in return for a mortgage; and if the mortgage
was overdue, he foreclosed without mercy.
The bad seasons, thus, instead of reducing
his income rather increased it, for it enabled
him to sell out a lot of his customers, who
henceforth became his tenants, and depen-
dent upon him for their food and the roof
over their heads.

He now began to fit out boat-guilds for
cod-fishing, hiring the men, and giving them
a small share of the profits. But he understood to perfection the art of driving hard
bargains; and somehow, whether the fisher-
men who were tossed about on the sea in
cold and wet weather earned anything or
not, Prebensen always managed to save himself, and set apart a margin of profits.

Like a big spider, he sat in his office and
threw out his toils over the town, until there
was scarcely anybody outside of the circle
of government officials who was not more
or less involved in his web.

For the members of the government circle
he professed the greatest respect. When he
had moved away from the back street, and
established himself in roomier and more re-
spectable quarters, he went south to Bergen,
and returned with a wife whose family had
extensive connections in the whaling and
sealing trade.

He now began a social campaign, which
ended with the surrender of the pastor, the
major commanding the fortress, and all
others who belonged to the official circles.
They had formerly looked down upon him,
and had taken the part of Mr. Vang, who
was certainly a gentleman, and whose dinner-
parties and balls had, in earlier days, been
the great events of the winter.

But now Mr. Vang had all he could do in
keeping himself on his legs. He could no
longer afford to give balls and dinner-parties ;

and as Prebensen could, the people of qual-
ity who loved amusement gradually deserted
from the one to the other.

The " Petrel " had been launched as a last
desperate hope by Mr. Vang. One or two
successful voyages might restore his fortunes,
and enable him to give his children the education which was their just due, for they were
both more than ordinarily gifted. Ingomar,
the boy, who was then ten or eleven years
old, had an excellent head for mathematics
and mechanics, and delighted in nothing so
much as the making of miniature ships and
machines full of ingenious contrivances.

The father meant with the proceeds of the
" Petrel's " voyages to send Ingomar to a
technical institute in France where he would
have an opportunity to develop his talent
to its full value. But, unhappily, in order
to equip the " Petrel " for the expedition, and
moreover pay his taxes, which were considerable, he was obliged to mortgage the
ship.

As it was held to be very disreputable to
bid at a tax-sale, — which was regarded as a

mere formality, — Mr. Vang chose to mortgage the "Petrel" for his taxes, and his
house for the equipment of the ship. For,
if lose he must, he would rather lose the
house than the "Petrel." He felt confident
that if the worst came to pass, the sheriff
would, as was his wont, make a nominal bid
at the auction, and knock it down to himself;
which only meant that whenever Mr. Vang
could conveniently pay the taxes, he could
have the sale cancelled, and in the mean
while he could let the ship sail and do with
it as he liked.

Such was the lax custom in those regions;
as, in fact, all over Norway. But in this
instance Mr. Vang found, to his grief, that
he had made a miscalculation. When the
auction had to be held, for Mr. Vang was
desperately short of funds, and the sheriff
had made his nominal bid of one thousand
dollars, Prebensen stepped boldly up to the
bar and cried, " Two thousand ! "

The . consternation in the auction-room
when that bid was made challenges description. Every man looked at his neighbor, as

if he thought the world was coming to an
end; and the sheriff, who stood on his platform with the hammer in his hand, was
stupefied.

"Did I hear an offer of two thousand
dollars?" he finally asked. "I suppose it
was a mistake."

"No mistake about that," answered Prebensen. "I said two thousand dollars, and
I'll say it again."

"But, my dear sir," remonstrated the
sheriff, "it is contrary to all custom — "

"Don't you bother about that!" inter-
rupted the merchant. "I know the law,
and I know what I am doing."

"But — but — the ship is worth ten times
as much at the very least!" ejaculated the
officer, with indignation.

"All right! you bid her up if you like,"
replied Prebensen, coolly.

But the sheriff was a poor man; and as he
had not remotely contemplated such a pur-
chase, he might only involve himself in diffi-
culties, and incur Prebensen's hostility to
boot. It was the latter possibility which

silenced him; for the consul was an ugly
customer when he chose to make himself
disagreeable. It took a braver man than the
sheriff to thwart him in a plan upon which he
had obviously set his heart.

So it happened that the " Petrel," just as
she was about to restore the fortunes of the
house of Vang, took the wrong tack and
swelled instead the fortunes of its enemy,
Prebensen.

There was no use denying it. Prebensen
was now the big man of the town. He was
richer than all the rest put together. Vang
had been pushed to the wall; he had failed,
lost everything he had, and now carried on
a modest little business as a junk-dealer and
provisioner of ships.

He had never tried to revenge himself on
Prebensen. Nay, though he heartily de-
spised him, he made no show of enmity.
The town was so small that an open feud
would have resulted in innumerable unpleas-
antnesses, and would have caused incon-
venience and detriment to all. Mr. Vang
thought he owed it to the community in

which he lived to conceal his feelings, and
simply appear to acknowledge that Mr.
Prebensen — now Consul Prebensen — had
ousted him in honest competition.

The " Petrel," as she dropped her anchor
in the middle of the harbor, and lay gently
rocking over her own pretty image, had
evidently a good conscience, in spite of all
the mischief she had wrought. The consul,
with his daughter Ragna, was standing in
his gig at the end of the pier, waiting for
his son Sophus, who was to accompany them
out to the barque.

Mr. Prebensen was a small, thin, wiry man,
with a sharp, clean-shaven face. He had
small, shrewd, steel-blue eyes, and a mouth
that shut like a steel trap. The expression
in his features was usually stern ; but in his
eyes there was an alert, secretly watchful
look, like that of a fox or weasel that has
to be circumspect in order to make a living.
You saw at once that he was not a man who
would be caught napping.

His daughter, who was standing at his
side, did not resemble him. She was four-

teen years old, but tall for her age. What was most noticeable about her was the free and fearless manner in which she carried her head, and the two long yellow braids that hung down her back. Her face was fresh and rosy, her hair a trifle curly, and her eyes were full of mirth.

"Papsty," she said, — for by this jocose name she was wont to address her father, — "let us go without Sophus. He is always late. You know it takes him as many hours to make his toilet as it takes me minutes."

"It might not be bad if you paid more attention to those things," replied the consul, severely.

"Oh, pshaw!" cried Ragna, with a toss of her head. "But look! there is Ingomar. Let us take him along. He is such good fun. Come here, Ingomar; don't you want to row out to the 'Petrel'?"

The boy, though he felt that his dignity rebelled, could not resist so tempting an invitation. To go on board the "Petrel;" to mouse around in all her lockers and chests and cabins, with all the fascinating foreign smells; to hear the **story of her voyage at first hand,** — the thought **of such** delights made **him dizzy.**

So he slipped quietly **into the boat, and made** himself as small as possible for fear of getting into collision with the consul. The latter **had not** heard his daughter's invitation, being absorbed in his own calculations; and as he caught sight of Ingomar, seated **on the** thwart, said, with a snarl, —

"Get out of here! Who has **asked** you, I should like to know?"

"I have asked **him, papsty,"** his **daughter** replied; "he is my guest, and **I want you to** be nice to him."

Ingomar was much inclined to step ashore again, and would have done so if Ragna had not put her hand on his shoulder and said, **"I** want you to go with us, Ingomar. I shall **be offended** with you **if you** don't stay."

Ingomar could not resist such a gentle appeal. He felt how all **the boys on the** pier envied him, as he sat there **in the fine** black-painted gig with the red line under the gunwale, and he saw presently that there

was going to be a struggle to follow his
example.

" Hi, there, missy ! " a little street Arab
called out; "take me along, won't you?"

Ragna shook her head smilingly.

" Oh, do take me along, Miss Ragna ! " another boy begged; " my dad is on board, and
I hain't seen him for nigh onto half a year."

She knew the boy, and kind-hearted as
she was, she found it impossible to refuse
him. His father, Tobias Trulson, was second
mate of the " Petrel." So she nodded her
head; and Thomas, eager for any signal of
acquiescence, tumbled headlong into the gig.
The boat gave a lurch; the consul lost his
balance, and would have gone overboard if
one of the oarsmen had not caught hold of
him.

" Have you lost your wits, boy?" he
cried, white with anger; " or do you think I
can take all the ragamuffins in town along
with me?"

Starting forward, he gave the boy a kick
which sent him headlong into the water.

Just at that moment the consul's son,

Sophus, dressed in the height of fashion,
made his way through the crowd; that is,
he lifted up his cane imperiously and commanded the people to open lane for him.
The people, though growling among themselves, fell apart obediently and let the young
gentleman walk unmolested through their
midst.

This incident seemed so much more important than the mishap to little Thomas
Trulson, that scarcely any one troubled himself about the manœuvres of the second
mate's son. As ill luck would have it, he
came up, the first time, under the gig and
bumped his head against her keel; and
though he was a good swimmer, the shock
confused him so that he did not know in
what direction he was moving.

As Sophus, redolent of Jockey Club,
stepped into the boat, Ingomar heard dis-
tinctly the bump against the bottom of the
boat, and leaning over the gunwale, saw, to
his horror, that the boy was sinking, and,
bent double with cramps, was unable to
direct his movements through the water.

Help was needed here, and needed quickly. Without a moment's hesitation, Ingomar
flung off his coat and waistcoat and leaped
over the gunwale. The shock of the icy
bath was so great that it almost stunned
him.

" Go ahead ! " commanded the consul; and
when the oarsmen seemed reluctant, he
added lightly: " Vang's boy will pick up the
little ragamuffin, and so we are rid of both
of them. You take my word for it," he continued, with an unpleasant laugh; " they will
scramble out. Weeds of that kind are
tough. The more you trample on them
the better they thrive. Neither fire nor
water will kill 'em."

The bright oars struck the water with
strong, rapid strokes, and the gig shot out
over the shining surface of the sound. The
consul and his son chatted carelessly, and
the son struck a storm-match and lighted
a cigarette. But Ragna, with a face tense
with excitement, stood up in the stern and
gazed toward the head of the pier. At last,
when she saw Ingomar hand up the stiff and

crooked little creature to a man in a boat, and himself ascend the stairs to the pier, dripping wet and half frozen, she flung herself down in the bottom of the gig and wept as if her heart would break.

"Oh, father," she cried, "how could you do it? How could you do it?"

"Don't be a goose, daughter!" said the consul, with the same little snarl in his voice; "don't waste your tears on such trifles."

INGOMAR SAVES LITTLE THOMAS.

CHAPTER II.

TOBIAS TRULSON, late second mate of the
" Petrel," was sitting in his small cottage,
which smelled of smoked salt fish and wet
clothes; but Tobias was so accustomed to
that smell that he did not mind it. In fact,
he would have missed it if it had been absent. A peat fire was smouldering upon a
hearth built of rough stones, and a pine
knot, stuck into a crevice in the wall, was
crackling and flickering, and throwing an
unsteady light over the miserable interior.

A long fishing-net hung in festoons along
the walls, — for Tobias was going to mend
it as soon as he got time, — and on a line
under the ceiling were wet clothes hung up
to dry. People up in that Arctic wilderness
are usually wet, and a good deal of their

time is taken up in the effort to get dry. They have to extract their scanty living from the vast, wild Polar Sea, and if generations of struggle and hardship had not toughened them, they would perish miserably in the course of one winter.

Tobias Trulson was one of the toughest and hardiest of this tough and hardy race. He was a large, brawny man, with a deeply wrinkled, weather-beaten face of coppery color, and a head of thick brown hair, which looked as if the wind had been playing the mischief with it. It seemed to grow the wrong way above the ears, and it had, moreover, a curious " ripple," as the sea has under a light breeze.

" You say he kicked you overboard? " said the mate to his small son, whom he was holding in his lap. The boy had an ugly cut on his forehead where he had struck the keel of Prebensen's gig. His little fists were tightly clinched, and his eyes had a strange glow in the unsteady light. His father, half forgetting his question, sat staring at him with a troubled look. Now and then he put his hand on the lad's hot forehead, and felt his rapid pulse hammering away in his temples.

"And you say he kicked you overboard, sonny?" Tobias repeated, after a while.

"Yes, he did, pop," piped the child, feebly nodding his tousled head.

"And you had n't been doin' nothin' to him, Tom?"

The boy panted for a moment before he found his voice. "I jumped into his boat," he said, with chattering teeth, "'cos the girl asked me."

Tobias fell into a deep meditation. At the end of fifteen minutes, during which he had been staring fixedly into the fire, he arose, and shaking his clinched fist toward the ceiling, cried, —

"I'll pay him back for that some day!"

His wife, Karen, who had been sitting in a corner patching a pair of small trousers that seemed beyond the stage of profitable patching, started up with a frightened face, and putting her hand on his arm, implored him to make no such rash threats.

" You know we are poor people, Tobias,"
she said, " and we depend upon the consul
for everything. We can't afford to quarrel
with our bread and butter."

" I 'd rather starve than eat his bread any
more," growled Tobias; " and as for the butter, I have never had so much as a taste
of it !"

" Yes, but the children ! Have you a right
to let them starve too in order to gratify
your own spite?"

" Oh, the children ! the children !" groaned
the mate. " What a coward they have made
of me! They tie my tongue and they tie
my hands !"

" Bless their dear little hearts !" said the
literal Karen; " they could n't do that if
they tried."

An infant wrapped in rags, which rested
in her lap, here began to whimper; and she
hugged it to her bosom, hushing it with fond
words, as if to defend it against its father's
insinuations.

" Anyway, I should like to know what we
have to thank Prebensen for," the mate went

on, after a pause. "I have been a-workin'
myself to skin and bones these ten years to
make him rich, and what do I get fur it?
Well, now I come home after five months
of starvin' and freezin' and hard usage, and
not a cent do I find is due to me. My
family has eaten up my wages, the clerk tells
me, and it is me as owes Prebensen, and not
Prebensen as owes me. Now, ef thar's sense
in that, you jest call me a jackass and be
done with it."

With an angry scowl he looked about in
the poor room, at the rags which had been
stuffed into the window-sashes where the
panes had been broken, at the worn and
rickety floor which creaked when one walked
on it, and at the alcove in the wall where
four children slept on a bed made of straw
and dried seaweed. Two of them, who were
given to kicking off their covering in the
night, had been tied up in coffee-bags, —
marked "Java No. 2" in big letters, —which
had been fastened about their necks.

"When you sailed in Vang's ships,"
Karen observed, rocking the baby to and

fro, " it was different. Then we always came out ahead."

" Yes, and God bless him for all he did for me and mine ! " exclaimed Tobias, fervidly. " It 's hard, it 's mighty hard, that such a man must go to the bottom fur to raise such a one as Prebensen. I don't understand it, — no, blest if I do ! "

The little boy, whose head had been resting wearily on his father's shoulder, now closed his eyes ; and Tobias, stealing on tiptoe across the floor, put him down in the second alcove, and covered him with an old coat. Resuming his seat before the fire, he began to cut up some plug tobacco in the palm of his hand and to stuff it into his pipe.

" Well, well," he said meditatively, blowing out a cloud of smoke, " I suppose the Lord knows what He 's about. I don't."

The mate fell into a brown study ; and little Thomas, who sat up wide awake the moment his father had turned his back on him, was vaguely wondering whether he meant to kill Prebensen or only to thrash

him, for Thomas knew no other methods of
retaliation. In the intervals of his fever it
flattered him to have kicked up such a rum-
pus, and he felt something like gratitude to
his father for having taken his part so warmly,
and grown so angry on his account.

The pain in his forehead could not prevent
him from imagining, in a dazed way, what
a hero he would be among the boys in
town when Tobias should have carried out
his threat, and he hoped in his heart that his
mother would not succeed in mollifying him.
He was aroused from this meditation by a
vigorous thump on the door. Tobias made
some slow preparations to rise, but before he
could reach the latch, the door was opened,
and a handsome curly head appeared in the
opening.

" May I come in, Tobias? " asked a merry
young voice.

Without awaiting the mate's reply, a tall,
slender lad of sixteen bounded into the
room. He came like a fresh breeze, and
the hopelessness which had reigned there a
moment before was as if blown away.

"Ingomar!" cried Tobias, joyously, grasping both the boy's hands. "Well, well, well! How big and handsome we have grown! I should n't have known ye hardly, if it had n't been fur them eyes of yourn, fur nobody never had eyes with such snap in 'em. And I was a-comin' round to see ye, Ingomar, my lad, and thank ye fur haulin' that unlucky little chap of mine out of the water when Prebensen kicked him overboard."

"Oh, never mind that!" answered Ingomar, with a toss of his head. "It was nothing."

"Well, it came mighty near bein' somethin', though," the mate remonstrated, choking a little as he spoke. "But I hain't simmered down enough to talk about it yet, so ye be right; it 's better to keep mum."

Ingomar flung his cap on a table which stood between the windows, and pulled a chair, made out of the vertebra of a whale, up to the fire.

"Well, old man," he said to Tobias, "I am glad to have you safe home again. I have missed you a good deal."

Tobias took three long pulls at his pipe before he replied.

"Thankee, Ingomar, thankee!" he said at last. "Ef I was a-sailin' fur your dad now, instead of that white-livered sneak as kicked my little chap into the water, I should be happier to get home, lad, than I am to-day."

"And what kind of voyage did you have, Tobias? That's what I came to ask you about. They say Prebensen is pretty badly cut up about something or other, and some think it is because the 'Petrel' has been losing money."

"They be n't far wrong as to that, lad. We've had a mighty bad voyage, — bad water, bad meat, and bad luck from the start. We lost more whales than we ever did in any three voyages before."

"Lost them? How did you lose them?"

"Two thirds of them sank as soon as we had killed 'em."

"What made them sink?"

"Bad luck, I guess. And then they were so lean! The Finmark whale is the strongest whale that swims in the sea. He takes

too much exercise to raise much fat, and it
is the fat makes him float. One monstrous
chap took us in tow fur ten hours, and I
don't know but he would have towed us
right on to the North Pole, if the line had n't
snapped."

"What did you do then?"

"What could we do? We had to let
him go."

"I should think something might be invented to prevent the whale from sinking,"
remarked Ingomar, thoughtfully.

"If ye can invent that, lad, then your fortune is made," answered Tobias; "but when
you have found it, hold on to it, and keep
mum till you have your patent in your
pocket."

"Trust me for that!" ejaculated the boy,
jumping up and pacing the floor, as was his
wont, when a new idea agitated him.

"It does seem feasible to me, Tobias," he
said, pausing abruptly in front of the sailor.

"It would have been worth twelve thousand dollars to Prebensen on this voyage
alone, if our skipper had known of such a

thing," the mate observed, knocking out his pipe on his boot-heel.

Ingomar seated himself again, and began a regular cross-examination of his host in regard to all the phases of whale-fishing. They were very old friends, and fond of each other. Tobias had taught Ingomar all he knew of marine lore. He had taught him how to row, swim, reef a sail, tack, jib, and steer, and the more intimate knowledge of his profession, such as weather-signs, good and bad indications for fishing; and the doings and peculiarities of the Ship-Brownie he had also imparted to his favorite pupil under the pledge of secrecy.

In the days of Mr. Vang's prosperity, when Tobias was a young fellow, he had felt not a little honored at being intrusted with this most important part of the young master's education, and had been an envied character in the town on account of the prospects which such a friendship opened up to him.

It was then freely hinted that Tobias knew on which side his bread was buttered; but Tobias put such slanderers to shame. He

was a stanch and **loyal soul, and as** devoted
to Vang **and his house in their adversity as**
he **had ever been in the days of their**
opulence.

The **two friends were so deeply absorbed**
in their discussion **of whaling that they did**
not hear a twice **repeated knock at the door.**
The third knock, **however, aroused Karen,**
who had **been** dozing **over the baby.   She**
went **to the door,** but **had no sooner opened**
it **than she started back in astonishment.**

" Have **you lost your way in the dark,**
miss," she **asked, "and do you want some-**
body to take **you home?"**

" Oh, not **at all! " a** cheerful voice answered.
" I came **to** ask **how the little** boy is who
— who — had the **mishap — who —** fell **into**
the water."

" **Oh,** he ain't dead, miss," Karen muttered
sullenly, " **and I** guess **he don't mean to**
gratify you **by dying."**

She was **about to shut the door in her**
visitor's face, **when Ingomar, who** had recog
nized Ragna's **voice, rose and** stayed her
hand.

"Let her come in," he said; "she is not to blame for the accident."

Karen, who was accustomed to think Ingomar infallible, stepped aside and let the young girl enter.

"Well, I'll be blowed!" was the greeting Tobias gave her. He did not rise, far less offer her his hand.

Ragna, though not expecting a cordial reception, became a trifle embarrassed and scarcely knew how to state her errand. Half absently she handed a basket which she carried on her arm to Ingomar, and walking over to the little boy, who was still sitting up in the alcove bed, she stooped down and patted his cheek.

"Why, you poor thing, you've got fever," she ejaculated, stroking his hair back from his forehead. "I brought you some nice things to eat and some toys for your little sister, — Anna, isn't that her name?"

The boy only stared at her with his big eyes, and did not answer.

"I didn't think you were so ill, Tom," Ragna went on, "or I should have brought

you medicines too; but I'll send the doctor
to you if you like."

Tom shook his head. "No, no doctor,"
he said.

"And won't you eat some smoked tongue
and some bread and butter? And I have got
some jam too."

All these delicacies would have been irre-
sistible to Tom at any other time; but just
then the pain in his head returned and di-
verted his thoughts from the temptation. He
fell back upon the sack which served for a
pillow, and groaned.

Tobias, who had only with difficulty contained himself, now jumped up and advanced
two long strides toward the young girl.

"What do ye come here for?" he asked
savagely.

"I felt sorry for the little boy," answered
Ragna, meeting his glance fearlessly.

"You jest obleege me by not feelin' sorry
fur me nur none of mine," he demanded, with
the same challenging mien; "ye ought to feel
sorry rather that ye have got a father as will
kick a little chap as has n't done him no harm."

RAGNA IN TRULSON'S COTTAGE.

"Tobias," cried Ingomar, stepping up to the mate and grabbing him by the arm, "shame on you! That is not fair."

But Tobias had boiled so long inwardly that he could not now be pacified.

"And was it fair," he yelled, "what Prebensen did to Tom this morning? If it had n't been for you, Tom would have been carried out dead with the tide. For five months I had worked and starved on board his ship, — fur he 's too mean to provision his ships as the law demands, — and when my little chap is anxious-like to come out and see his dad, he kicks him overboard as if he had been a nasty cur, and never even stops to see if he gets drownded. You call that fair, do you?"

"No, I don't," Ingomar retorted quietly; "but it was n't Ragna who did it. And I call it cowardly to take revenge on a girl for her father's doings."

"Cowardly! Cowardly, did you say? Did you call me cowardly?"

Beside himself with anger, Tobias raised his clinched fist; but Ingomar stood erect and fearless, staring at him with unflinching eyes.

"Yes," he repeated slowly, "I call your conduct cowardly. I always thought well of you, Tobias, and I believed you to be a man, with the courage of a man in your breast. But when you hurt so cruelly one who has come with pity in her heart to help you, I cannot call you my friend."

"I don't want her pity. I don't want the pity of any of her tribe," shouted the mate, threateningly.

"Well, then, tell her so quietly, but don't insult her," the boy responded gallantly.

"Well, I did n't have the bringin' up of a gentleman, and I don't pretend to be one. I am a plain man, and I speak bluntly as I feel."

The brunt of his wrath had spent itself, and he was beginning to feel ashamed of his violence. But just as his reason was about to assert itself, he caught sight of his wife stooping over Ragna's basket, and with a face full of furtive delight, unpacking its contents. There were a dozen or more slices of smoked tongue, at least twenty sandwiches, several loaves of bread, and a small jar of jam.

The poor starved woman, who had scarcely eaten anything but salt fish and tough, oily seal-flesh during her entire life, had not the courage to refuse such dainties. Her eyes blazed with eager anxiety to get the things put away before her husband should discover them.

But, unhappily, she was not quick enough. Like an angry animal he pounced upon her, wrenched the plate of sandwiches out of her hands, and opening a window pitched it into the street. Tongue, bread, cake, and jam went the same way, one after the other, and neither tears nor prayers were of any avail.

"Tobias, dear Tobias," the wife implored him, "we have nothin' in the house to eat, and you fling good victuals into the street for the dogs and the sea-gulls. Think of the children, Tobias. They have had nothing but herring and potatoes now for three weeks."

"I ain't sech a poltroon as to curse a

man and then eat his bread," was Tobias's
answer.

He was holding the empty basket in his
hand, and with angry energy he hurled it
through the window into the black night.

Ingomar, who had stood speechless at
Ragna's side, watching the mate's *Berserkir*
rage, picked up his cap, and beckoning to
the young girl, approached the door.

Poor Karen, who had some faint hope yet
of saving the precious food from the dogs,
went to the threshold with them, and was
about to accompany them further, under the
guise of politeness, when her husband, suspecting her design, rushed after her, seized
her by the arm, and dragged her back into
the room.

"Don't you dare to touch it!" he cried.
" I 'll show you I am master in my own
house ! "

A fierce wind was blowing outside, and it
was pitch-dark. Far away a luminous point
was visible, but it was quite insufficient to
dispel the darkness. Some rickety street-
signs creaked and screamed dismally in the

wind, and now and then the spray from the sea came hissing through the air and lashed the window-panes.

Round about the island — only seven miles in circumference — upon which the town was built the great Arctic Ocean roared, and with a perpetual boom of thunder charged in wrathful onsets, as if to engulf it. These hoarse howls of wrath filled the air through all the winter months, except on rare occasions, when the Sound between the island and the mainland was frozen over.

" Give me your hand, Ragna," said Ingomar, " or you will be blown out to sea."

" I was looking for my basket," shouted Ragna, for the wind nearly drowned her voice.

" You might as well look for that at the North Pole."

She groped her way with one hand along the wall of a fisherman's hut which turned the gable to the street; and Ingomar, who held her other hand, was guiding her through the darkness.

" I stayed longer than I intended," Ragna

remarked after a while; " I hope they won't
be anxious about me at home."

" But I suppose they know where you went."

" No, they don't. I got all the things
from the cook, and she thought I wanted to
eat them myself, or invite some girls to my
room."

They kept close in shelter of the houses;
but whenever they came to a street-crossing,
where the wind had full sweep, they had to
cling to each other in order to keep their
footing.

" I wish my father liked you better, Ingomar," said Ragna, when once more they had
gained the shelter of a house-wall.

" I don't like him any better than he likes
me," the boy was tempted to answer; but he
checked his tongue, and asked instead, —

" Why do you want him to like me
particularly?"

" Well — because then we could be friends
openly and not only on the sly."

Ingomar had nothing to answer to this,
and so they set their heads against the wind,
and struggled bravely onward.

"Ragna," he said, suddenly facing her and holding both her hands, "I won't mind telling you one thing, because you are my friend, but you must promise me never to tell it to anybody."

"Oh, you only trust me for that!" cried the girl enthusiastically, for she had a tremendous relish for secrets.

"Well, some day I am going to be a great man, and then it won't matter much what your — what anybody thinks of me. I feel it here — inside of me, Ragna," he went on, with a ring of strong conviction; "but I never dared tell it even to father, because I can't bear to be laughed at."

"Oh, but, Ingomar," exclaimed Ragna, flushed and flattered by his confidence, "I always thought you 'd be something great!"

"Did you really, Ragna?"

"Yes, I did."

"What made you think so?"

"Well, I don't know; I think it must be your eyes. There is a look in them which is — so good — and — and nice," she finished confusedly.

"Good and nice?" he repeated with obvious disappointment.

"Well, something that makes one believe in you, — which makes it impossible not to believe in you," she added eagerly.

She did not see how his face lighted up with pleasure at that sweet assurance. Something in his nature, finer than vanity, responded to those sympathetic words with joyous ardor.

He had led a lonely life, with his ambition, and had never known the delight of being understood and appreciated. Therefore Ragna's avowal sounded in his ears like the most intoxicating music. And it seemed to him almost miraculous that she had actually guessed his secret (which, for fear of ridicule, he had so carefully hidden from all), and suspected the greatness which he now more than ever believed to be within his reach.

The streets of Vardöe were at that time crooked and hilly, and lighted at long intervals by lamps swung on wires, which had a way of being blown out when the wind was high; and as the wind was generally high, the lamps were generally out of repair when they were most needed.

Ragna and Ingomar had just reached the top of the hill that leads toward the so-called West End, where the well-to-do citizens lived, when they saw half-a-dozen lights flickering to and fro across the street. Shouts, too, were borne toward them on the blast; and they concluded that some misfortune had happened. It did not occur to them to shout back, as they never dreamed that the summons was intended for them.

With a vague relish of the excitement, they started forward, eager to know the cause of the disturbance. They had scarcely advanced half a block, however, when Ragna stopped and stared with a frightened face at her companion.

"Ingomar," she exclaimed breathlessly, "they are hunting for *me!*"

"What makes you think so?"

"I hear them shout my name."

"You had better shout back, then, to let them know where you are."

"Yes, but you must leave me first, Ingomar. Father would n't like to see us together."

"Do you think I am a sneak?" cried the boy, proudly; "I won't run away from anybody!"

Two men with torches and two more with lanterns were now approaching; and Ingomar shouted to them with all his might, Ragna reluctantly joining. The foremost man in the line, in whom they presently recognized Prebensen, rushed forward the instant he heard their voices.

"Ho! ho!" he cried angrily, thrusting his lantern into their faces, "this is you, miss, is it? You have nearly frightened us out of our wits."

Ragna flushed as she saw the men standing about her, but made no answer.

"This is a nice time for promenading, is n't it?" her father continued sarcastically, curbing his wrath; "and you, young man," he went on, turning the full glare of the lantern on Ingomar, — "I 'll have a talk with you later."

Ingomar had a stinging reply ready, but out of regard for Ragna forbore to utter it. He only lifted his cap silently, and vanished in the darkness.

CHAPTER III.

IN a large room which had once served for a hay-loft Ingomar had his workshop. The stable, which had once housed half-a-dozen fine animals, was now inhabited by one ancient and sedate nag whose fodder was kept in a neighboring stall, and the remaining stalls were used by the young inventor for storage of his models and other treasures. For Ingomar was a boy to whom everything was of interest. He was indefatigably busy from morning till night.

He had been a trifle spoiled, perhaps, by his father, who had perfect confidence in him, and who found little time to occupy himself with his son's education.

Ingomar's mother had died four years ago, leaving a little daughter named Magda, who was now nine years old.

Four other sisters and brothers had died
in early infancy; for it takes a very strong
child to survive one of the terrible Arctic
winters, when for two months the sun never
peeps above the horizon, and storm and
darkness hold sway in the heavens above,
and on the earth below.

The room above the stable, where Ingomar
spent his happiest hours, was more like an
inventor's laboratory than an artisan's workshop. There was, to be sure, a turning-
bench in a corner, and a variety of tools
were visible in a rack on the wall. But the
most conspicuous object was a small hearth,
like that of a forge, with bellows and a chimney that pierced the roof. Ingomar had
partly built this himself, with the aid of a
mason's apprentice who was his friend.

Suspended under the roof and on shelves
about the walls were stuffed sea-birds of
many kinds, and seals, weasels, martens, and
foxes. For Ingomar's first enthusiasm, when
he was four years younger, had been tax-
idermy, and he had acquired considerable
skill in this art, and earned some money by

the sale of his finest specimens to English
and American tourists. In order to guard
against fire he had covered the floor with a
layer of crushed sea-shells, and the walls
with asbestos paper.

Here in this delightful room, which was all
his own, Ingomar was seated one morning,
about a month after his visit to Tobias Trulson. With one hand he was slowly working
the bellows, while in the other he held a
book on chemistry, in which he was eagerly
reading. A wooden model of a swivel-gun,
about a foot long, was standing on a table
near the window, illumined by two whale-oil
lamps which were attached to the wall.

The boy's face, as he turned it toward the
light, was blackened with soot and flushed
with excitement. His entire person, from
the chin down, was covered with a leathern
apron, such as smiths wear.

With an exclamation of impatience he
flung down the book and began to walk up
and down the floor. The light of the two
lamps did not radiate much beyond the
forge and the table, and all the rest of the

room was in twilight; for the dark season
had now begun, and all over the town the
window-shades were pulled down and the
yellow flames of the candles glimmered
all day long through the chinks of the
shutters.

It was bitter cold without, and the wind
swept fiercely around the corners of the
house. The steady humming of the stove
sometimes rose to a roar, and sometimes
ceased suddenly when the wind dashed down
the chimney and flung a fiery tongue from
the draught-hole out into the room.

The ice on the window-panes was almost
thick enough to make the shades superfluous, and the cotton batting which had
been stuffed into the chinks, and the ser-
pentine sand-bags which guarded against
draughts, were covered with half an inch of
hoar-frost.

Ingomar stopped abruptly in his march,
and stared with kindling eyes at his gun
model. " I have it! " he cried joyously, and
made a leap across the floor. " A bomb is
the thing! Hurrah for the bomb! "

He was so absorbed that he failed to hear the creaking of the stairs and the sound of heavy footsteps. But he could not fail to hear the thump on the door, which nearly shook it out of its frame; nor fail to see the big, brawny figure in oil-clothes which presently filled the doorway.

"Who's there?" cried Ingomar, anything but happy to be disturbed.

"It's me," answered a voice out of the dusk.

"Well, what do you want, Tobias?" asked Ingomar, instantly recognizing the voice.

The broad, weather-beaten figure lumbered forward, and pulling off a huge mitten, stretched out a dark-brown, horny paw.

"Let us be friends, lad," he said, when Ingomar hesitated to grasp his hand. "I can't get along without you; you can't get along without me."

"Don't be so sure of that, Tobias," the boy answered; "if you are so violent as you were the other night, I don't know but I should be better off without you."

"Don't say that, lad, don't say it!"

pleaded the mate. " I reckon I was pretty
nasty, and I feel mighty mean about it now.
But you and me — we was sorter growed
up together — though it was you as did the
growing; but I have been so miserable sence
you turned your back on me that I'll do
anything you like, only so as we be friends
as we was afore."

Ingomar looked up into the sailor's big,
coppery face, and its deeply troubled look
touched him.

" All right, Tobias ! " he said, now pressing
his hand, which felt like a piece of tanned
leather; "we'll let bygones be bygones."

"Thankee, lad, thankee! It do make a
new man of me to see ye brightenin' up a
bit."

" Sit down, Tobias; you can talk while I
work. I have a little experiment here which
I can't very well drop."

" Let's have a look at it."

" Mind you, mum's the word, Tobias."

" Don't you be afeard of me, sonny; I ain't
the blabbin' kind."

The boy pulled a small harpoon out of the

smouldering fire on the hearth, and in his eagerness thrust it up under the mate's nose. Tobias started back, but recovered himself and began to inspect the weapon.

" That is n't made right," said he.

" Just so," ejaculated Ingomar; " that 's just the point."

" Why have you made it hollow? "

" Listen to me, Tobias. You know you said a third of the whales caught, on an average, went to the bottom, and that this third was apt to make the difference between profit and loss. Now, this harpoon is made hollow, because it is to contain a bomb, which, when it explodes, will generate gas; and this gas will buoy the whale up and prevent him from sinking."

" But who 's to explode the bomb? Ye can't get inside the whale with a fuse or anything of that kind."

" The whale himself is to explode it. The rope which is attached to the harpoon is to be connected with a wire running through the hollow shaft, and the first pull the whale gives will burst the bomb and fill his insides

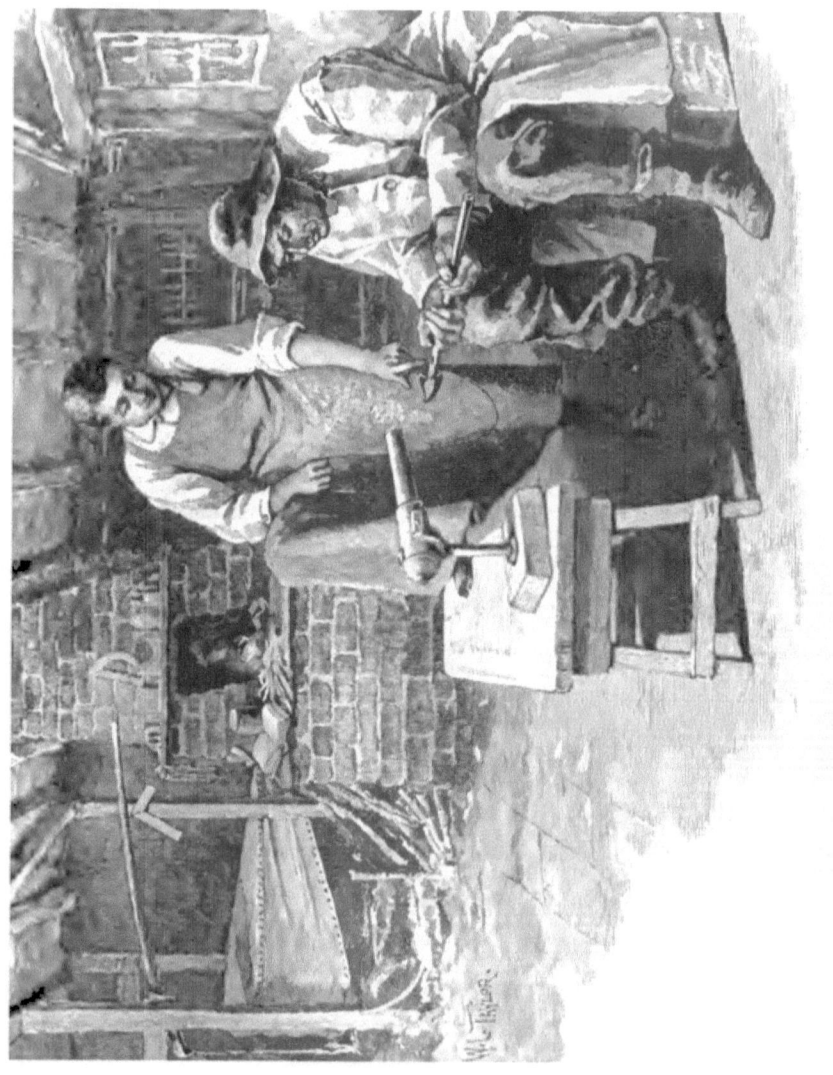

THE HARPOON GUN.

with a gas which will make his huge, lumbering carcass ten per cent lighter."

The young inventor, carried along by his ideas, gazed in joyous excitement at his friend, challenging him with his eager eyes to find more objections if he could. The mate in the mean while scratched his head meditatively, and looked, half embarrassed, about the walls.

" Now, supposin' that is all right," he began at last, " who is to fire yer light harpoon, which, mind ye, is hollow, so far into the whale's body that it 'll stick? No human critter is strong enough for that."

" This ! " cried Ingomar, proudly, jumping up and putting his hand on his model of the swivel-gun. " I put the harpoon into the muzzle of the cannon and shoot it out with gunpowder."

" Wal, wal, wal! " exclaimed Tobias, in rapt astonishment. " If ye be n't the smartest lad I ever clapped eyes on! "

He began to examine the gun with profound interest, while Ingomar took it apart and explained the working of each detail.

There was one great hitch yet, he remarked, and that was to find the proper kind of gas, and the proper way of developing it. But he had no doubt but that by diligent experimenting he would succeed in finding precisely what he needed.

He had sold half his collection of stuffed birds and even his precious blue fox, and bought chemicals with the proceeds. Another month of study would, he hoped, perfect his invention; and then he would have a model made in steel, and send to Christiania to get his patent and make his fortune. For no whaler could henceforth afford to go to sea without Vang's Patent Harpoon Gun, and thus the fortunes of the house of Vang would rise Phœnix-like from its ashes, and the whole Finmark district would flourish as never before.

This was the dream which the enthusiastic boy had nursed in his solitude; and as he now related it to his friend, his eyes beamed with zeal and delight, and his voice shook with emotion. Tobias, though he was naturally doubtful about the success of so daring a plan, had not quite the heart to offer further objections. He only scratched his head meditatively as before.

After having once more examined the gun, he rose to take his leave.

" By the way, how 's little Tom ? " inquired Ingomar. " I hope he 's better."

" Oh, he 's tolerably middlin'. He 's been havin' pneumonia, but I reckon he 's goin' to pull through, if he only had enough to eat, poor chap ! "

" Has n't he enough to eat ? "

Tobias twirled his cap thoughtfully; then looking up with some embarrassment, said : " Why, Master Ingomar, there ain't anybody down in our part of town as has enough to eat. Some days, when we can put to sea and catch some fish or kill a seal, we manage to keep soul and body together; but when the weather is too rough, as it generally is at this season, we have to starve."

" But can't you get credit at Prebensen's ? "

" No; Prebensen won't give credit any more unless a man 's got something to mortgage. And pretty much all the town is mortgaged to him by this time — down our way."

"Come along with me, Tobias; though we haven't much ourselves, nowadays, I'll get you something. The trouble is, every one who is refused at Prebensen's comes to us; and father is too soft-hearted to send anybody away empty-handed."

They descended the stairs together, and passed through the stable into the courtyard. The wind had now gone down; the sky was glittering with innumerable stars, and the aurora borealis flashed its pink and yellow sheets of light from the horizon toward the zenith.

Though it was but a little after noon, not a ray of sunlight was anywhere visible; but for all that, there was a dazzling splendor in the scene which the sun could scarcely have rivalled. Each separate star twinkled and shone with an intenser brilliancy than it ever attains in our temperate zone; and the Milky Way, with its myriad luminous hosts, poured down upon the earth a flood of radiance.

Ingomar and his friend entered by the back door a rather shabby store, pervaded with the odor of tar and salt fish. Big barrels filled with salt mackerel and herring stood before the counter; coils of rope lay under the shelves; and green, brown, and yellow boxes were stowed away in little square compartments, exhibiting a sample nail, or screw, or fish-hook.

It was an unpretentious country-store, where you might without impropriety ask for anything from a suit of oil-clothes to a bottle of medicine.

There was a shrill little bell over the door, which announced each customer that entered or departed, and kept up a needless racket after the door was closed.

"Father," cried Ingomar to an elderly man with a kindly, careworn face, who stood writing at a desk, "Tobias says his children have nothing to eat. Have n't we got something to give him?"

"My dear boy," answered his father, looking up from his writing, "we shall soon be no better off than Tobias. I have given

away the better part of my stock because
the distress of the people moved me. Now
I can get credit no more myself, and then
there's an end of everything."

The boy gazed at the mournful face of
his father, and his grief cut him to the heart.
Why should he allow him to be sad when he
had it in his power to cheer him? He had
always looked up to him, believing him to
be the noblest of men.

"Father," he said, stepping up to the
older man and putting his hand affection-
ately on his shoulder, "what would you say
if I told you that some day you would again
be the richest man in Vardöe?"

Mr. Vang, feeling the enthusiasm which
trembled in his voice, gave a start of surprise, but in the next moment smiled sadly
and answered, —

"I should say, my dear, that you had
been dreaming. I have been routed in
the fight, and the hard part of it is that I
have been routed by foul means which I
would never condescend to use in return. A
scoundrel has that advantage over an hon-

est man, that he can fight him with weapons which his enemy would scorn to make use of."

"But you only wait, father," ejaculated the boy, with blazing eyes, "and *we'll* fight *him* with a weapon which he won't have the wit to make use of."

"What kind of a weapon is that?"

"A swivel-gun."

"My dear boy! I hope you are joking."

"Not at all. It is a new kind of harpoon gun I have invented."

"But, Ingomar, my son," cried Mr. Vang, with alarm in his face, "you surely are not thinking of doing him bodily harm?"

"Bodily harm! No, indeed!"

Ingomar flung his head back and burst into a ringing peal of laughter. "Why, father," he shouted, "you did n't imagine I wanted to harpoon Prebensen, did you?"

"Well, what else was I to suppose?"

The son had to have his laugh out; and Tobias, as soon as he saw the point, had to join him.

" I would n't mind myself havin' a crack at him," said the mate, " and I should n't have half as much on my conscience as he has. How many a ship he has sent to sea knowing her to be nothin' but a floatin' coffin! And when the news came that she had gone down, the widders put on weeds and the children cried for bread, and he let 'em starve, and pocketed ten or twenty thousand dollars' insurance for killin' them. It don't seem somehow right to be livin' quietly in a world where such things do happen. There's his brig, the ' Walrus,' a rickety old consarn that had been condemned ; but he manages somehow to get certificates of seaworthiness, and sends her with whalebone and oil to Hull."

Mr. Vang, without making any reply, beckoned the mate aside, put up a loaf of bread and other provisions in a package, and bade him good-by.

" Do you know, Ingomar," he said to his son as he returned to his desk, " I have sometimes thought it my duty to warn Prebensen."

"I would n't do anything of the sort!" ejaculated Ingomar, hotly.

"I am not so sure of that," his father answered thoughtfully. "He does not come in contact with the people as I do, and he does not know how they feel toward him."

"Then let him take the consequences of his own misdoings."

"If he were the only one who would suffer, perhaps that might not be out of the way; but the fact is, the whole town suffers. The welfare of all is in the hands of that one wretched man."

They walked into the dining-room and sat down to lunch. When they had finished eating, Ingomar took his skates and a pitch torch, ready for lighting, and persuaded his father to go with him down on the ice. The old gentleman, who loved nothing better than his son's society, was readily coaxed to lock up the store; and wrapped from head to foot in fur-lined overcoats, they started out together.

The moon had now risen, and showed its calm, bright face above the eastern horizon.

Though the air was still, a kind of icy
breath rose from the ground with a tomb-
like chill in it which penetrated all garments.
Father and son walked rapidly through the
quiet streets down toward the frozen harbor,
whence they heard snatches of song and
shouts of merriment. On account of the
tides and currents it was not often that the
Sound froze hard enough for skating, and
young people would not allow such an opportunity for enjoyment to escape them.

Toward the north the aurora borealis was
blazing and shooting forth long, fan-like
beams which swept across the sky. In this
magic illumination the ice lay outspread like
a huge steel-blue mirror, reflecting the ruddy
sheen of torches and the swiftly moving figures of boys and girls.

It was a very pretty sight, and Ingomar's
heart gave a bound of delight. With a shout
he leaped down the steps of the pier, flung
off his overcoat, fastened his skates on his
feet, lighted his torch, and darted out upon
the glittering surface.

His father remained standing on the pier,

watching with admiration his dexterous turns
and daring gyrations. Suddenly, like a flash,
while he was going at full speed, he flung
himself about and darted away backward in
undulating lines, swinging his torch about his
head, and challenging every boy on the ice
to race with him.

He found presently that some one had
accepted his challenge; but it was not a
boy, — it was Ragna Prebensen.

She wore a blue hood edged with swan's-
down, and a tight-fitting cloak of the same
color, lined with ermine.

"Ingomar," she said breathlessly, stretch-
ing out her hand to him, "why do you run
away from me?"

"I thought we were racing," he answered.

"You did n't think anything of the sort,"
she replied, with an injured air.

"Well, you know you and I are not to
talk to each other," he remarked, after a
pause.

"You need n't talk if you don't want to;
but we are going to have a torchlight quadrille on skates. Will you dance with me?"

Ingomar was greatly tempted to accept the invitation given so frankly and with such sincerity.

" But your father will not like it," he urged dubiously.

" Leave that to me; I 'll make it up with my father."

" All right, then; here I am."

He seized her hand, fell quickly into step with her, and darting rhythmically to the right and to the left, carried her along at such speed that the ice looked like a series of white and blue lines which came rushing madly toward them.

"Hurrah, this is life! " cried Ingomar, whirling his torch in the air so that the sparks flew like fiery snakes about them.

" Take care, you 'll singe my hood! " she cried.

" Oh, never mind the hood! "

They came to a standstill in the middle of the Sound, where about thirty or forty young people stood ready to begin the dance. The boys were dressed in short, fur-trimmed jackets and fur caps, and carried lighted torches.

" Hurrah, there is Ingomar!" cried a chorus of voices. " You lead, Ingomar, with Ragna Prebensen."

" All right!" said Ingomar. " Take your places! and you, girls, will commence the song when I raise my torch like this."

In five minutes more the boys and girls were arranged in two long lines on the ice, and at a signal from Ingomar the girls began to sing. It was the dance known in Norway as the Française, in which any number of couples may participate. It resembles in its figures the Lancers, or an enlarged quadrille, in which there are many couples, instead of one, on each side of the square.

The older people, who stood on the piers or promenaded along the shore, enjoyed the beautiful sight from a distance. The flickering torches, with their long, trembling reflections, the variegated lines of the dancers skating forward and backward to the rhythm of the song, the steely flash of the skates, the vast glittering surface of the ice, and the great dark-blue dome of the sky united into a picture to be remembered.

Mr. Vang, after having watched with pride
his son's skill as a skater, began to walk
up and down on the pier, in order to keep
his blood in motion. He had just reached
the sea-booths from which the pier projected,
when by chance he found himself face to face
with Consul Prebensen. His first impulse
was to pass him by without appearing to
observe him; but Tobias's story about the
"Walrus," and many similar stories which he
had heard from other quarters, inclined him
rather to seek an interview with his enemy.

"Good-day, Consul," he said, lifting his
cap.

"Good-day, Mr. Vang!" the consul replied, with an air of condescension. "I
hope you are well, sir," he added, holding
out two fingers, which Mr. Vang found it
prudent to press.

They talked for a few minutes about indif-
ferent things; and when once the ice was
broken, Vang steered skilfully toward the
subject which he had at heart.

"I hope you won't take it ill, Consul," he
said, "but as an older man, who had the

honor of being your first employer, I may perhaps be permitted to speak to you frankly."

Prebensen growled something in return which might be taken either for permission or refusal.

" You do wrong, Consul," Vang continued warmly, " in treating your sailors so harshly. You get your wealth out of their labor. I think you would find it for your own profit to extend their credit in bad years like the present. A man of your wealth and position can't afford to let men starve at his door."

" Mr. Vang," Prebensen replied, staring at his former employer with a pinched, ugly look, " I shall be obliged if you'll leave me to manage my business for myself. I pay my people what I agree to pay them. They don't work for me for nothing. They are at liberty to go elsewhere, if they can secure better terms."

" Well, what does that liberty amount to, Mr. Prebensen? You are now the only man here who owns ships and is rich enough to fit out boat-guilds for the fisheries. The people are too poor to go elsewhere, and you practically make your own terms."

" I don't do business on sentimental principles," the consul made haste to answer. " You tried that, and we all see the result. I am a practical man, and regard only business principles."

" But remember, Mr. Prebensen," Vang rejoined, ignoring the offensive allusion, " they are God's creatures; they are human beings like you and me."

" Indeed! Well, they may be like you, but they are not like me!" snarled the consul.

" Take care, Consul, take care!" cried Vang, earnestly. "I have given you warning. If you disregard it, you will live to rue it. These poor people whom you despise are, if they unite, a hundred times stronger than you. They are now at your mercy, but the day may come when you will be at their mercy."

CHAPTER IV.

A THORNY PATH.

AN inventor's path is not strewn with roses. Ingomar discovered, to his chagrin, that without money he would never be able to test the worth of his invention. He had, after months of steady experimenting, found the substances he needed for the generation of gas in his bomb, and felt confident that his gun would prove a success.

But in order to prove this he would have to have his model reproduced in steel, which would cost upward of two hundred dollars. Such a sum his father had not at his disposal; and however much he might strain his credit, he would scarcely be able to raise it. It even seemed to Ingomar, in moments of bitterness, that his father did not fully believe in his invention, but only humored him for fear of hurting his feelings.

There was not another soul in whom the poor boy dared confide; and the longer he brooded over his disappointment the sadder he grew.

One morning in June, when there was a feeling of spring in the air, he was roaming over the rocks, gun in hand, pondering on the subject which now never left his mind. The wary seals raised their round heads out of the water and gazed at him, or lay sunning themselves on the skerries, ready to plump into the sea if he should make any suspicious motion. But the young hunter strode away, with his head bent, without heeding them.

He had walked along for a couple of miles and was far outside the town, when he thought he heard his name called. He stopped, looked about him, but saw nothing except the black rocks, with patches of white and blue and yellow wild-flowers scattered between.

"Ingomar!" a voice called again, and it seemed to him that it was a girl's voice. He answered with a loud halloo. Presently, after another search, he discovered a yellow head which disentangled itself from a patch of yellow daffodils.

The sunlight was so dazzlingly bright that his eyes ached; and the sea, which broke with gentle murmurs at his feet, was like a huge burnished shield which reflected and intensified the light.

"Wait a moment! I want to see you," the yellow head called out from among the daffodils.

Ingomar paused and stood leaning on his gun. He knew well enough that the voice was Ragna's, but he yet feigned a little surprise at seeing her in such an out-of-the-way place. She was flushed and out of breath; and her loose hair was blown all over her face, giving her a resemblance to an obstinate little Shetland pony that is aware of its attractiveness and accustomed to have its own way.

"Well, you are the provokingest boy I ever knew," said Ragna, putting down a basket of flowers which she carried on her arm and seating herself on a big bowlder.

"I? How so?" queried Ingomar.

"Well, I have screamed till I am as hoarse as a crow. You must have heard me for the last fifteen minutes."

"You are mistaken. I answered you the moment I heard you."

"Well, we won't quarrel about it. But say, Ingomar, when are you going to be a great man? You remember you told me. I have been waiting for it daily, and I believe that is what makes me so out of breath," she added, coughing, and wiping her forehead with her handkerchief.

She glanced up at him, her eyes dancing with mischief.

"Ragna, you always were a great tease," he said with a sad smile; "but I beg of you, don't tease me on that subject."

"Why not?"

"Because I am very sensitive. You don't want to hurt me, do you?"

She grew suddenly serious, and a warm sympathy replaced the mischief in her eyes. "Look here, Ingomar," she said, "you have got some trouble. Tell me all about it."

"I can't, Ragna. You would n't understand it."

"Understand it! Well, I like that!" she
cried defiantly. "Now you 've *got* to tell
me. You might just as well give up at
once, for you won't have peace until you
do."

He forgot for the moment whose daughter
she was, and after some coaxing told her
his secret. It seemed very sweet to him,
after his long, solitary brooding, to pour
the tale of his struggles and disappoint-
ments into a sympathetic ear. The lively
interest which she betrayed in his ambition,
and her absolute confidence in his genius
were like balm to his wounded spirit.

"Ingomar," cried Ragna, when he had
finished his story, "I 'll tell you what to do.
You go to my father, and tell him what you
have told me. He will lend you the two
hundred dollars to make your model."

Ingomar gave an incredulous laugh and
looked out over the sea. He did not want
Prebensen's daughter to see the expression
of his face. She had no need of seeing it,

however, for she divined how her proposition would strike him.

"You don't know father," she continued eagerly. "He's a little gruff sometimes, and you would be, too, if you had so many bad people to try you as father has. But I can coax him to do anything I want him to do."

"That may be, but I don't want you to coax him to do anything for me," said Ingomar, proudly.

She rose abruptly, and with a toss of her head flung back her hair from her forehead. Why was he so foolishly proud and stubborn? Why did he make it so difficult for her to help him? She was disposed to resent the rebuff he had given her; but somehow, as she caught a glimpse of his handsome, mournful face, she could not find it in her heart to be angry with him.

"Now don't be rash, Ingomar," she begged, turning toward him a face full of sympathy and earnest pleading; "do allow me to help you. You know this is your only chance. I believe in you, and I'll make father believe in you too. I'll make him lend you the money, and help you to show the world what there is in you."

She sat down at his side on the rock and began coaxing him anew, using all her ingenuity and womanly arts to chase away his scruples; and the end of it was that he promised to go that very afternoon to the consul, explain to him his invention, and ask his aid.

Having accomplished this, Ragna picked up her basket, flung her hat on the back of her head, and with a shout ran down the hillside. He saw her presently emerge from among the rocks and push a wherry, which she had pulled up on the beach, into the sea as well as any man.

"She isn't a bad sailor, that girl!" he said to himself, as he turned his face homeward.

He had to battle with himself long and earnestly before he could make up his mind to seek an interview with Mr. Prebensen. If it had not been for his promise to Ragna, he would never have trodden the difficult path

up to the consul's big house. His wooden
model he carried in a neat box which he had
made for it, and the careful way in which he
handled it showed how precious it was to
him.

Three o'clock in the afternoon was the
hour which Ragna had fixed for the interview, for then her father would have finished
his after-dinner nap and lighted his cigar;
and she knew from experience that that was
the time when he was most likely to be ami-
able. In spite of these precautions, however,
Ingomar had his misgivings. As he walked
with slow, reluctant steps up the street, the
blood kept throbbing in his temples, and
he muttered to himself, "I wish I had n't
promised."

The houses in the shadow of which he
was walking were small, one and two story
wooden structures, with little garden-plots
in front of them, in which geraniums and
primroses were blooming.

The street was steep and the pavement
uneven. It was a shabby little town, certainly, steeped in whale-oil and the odor of

fish. But for all that, there was in this glorious spring weather a splendor of earth and sea and sky which made it almost beautiful. The sun, which now shone without interruption day and night, bathed the mean little houses in a strange rosy glow, which one would scarcely expect to see out of fairy-land.

It was odd, indeed; but this magical illumination was not without a certain influence upon Ingomar, as he climbed the steep hill, on the crest of which Prebensen's stately mansion was situated.

He felt himself like the prince in the fairy tale who had started out in search of adventures. Here under his arm he held the wonderful box which somehow was to make his fortune, and up there on the hill-top was the ogre's castle which he must invade. There was a princess in the case too; but she did not fit into the fairy tale, for she was fond of the ogre, and not at all inclined to chop his head off.

It was these fantastic thoughts which occupied the young inventor as he plodded along

toward the ordeal which was in store for him.
He rehearsed in his mind what he would say
to the consul; and imagined the questions
that would be put to him, and the answers
he would return. He was in the midst of
these speculations, when he suddenly ran
against an invisible barrier which scraped
his nose and knocked his hat off.

A burst of suppressed laughter and a
scurry of feet behind one of the houses told
him that the little street Arabs had played
a trick on him. A thin wire had been strung
across the street from one wall to another,
at about the proper height for knocking off
the hats of the passers-by.

Ingomar shook his fist laughingly at a
little rascal whom he saw peeping forth behind the corner; but made no attempt to
catch him. He was young enough to remember the time in his own life when such
tricks afforded him an exquisite pleasure.
He picked up his hat, and proceeded quietly
on his way. With a loudly beating heart he
entered Prebensen's store, and asked one of
the clerks if he might see the consul. He

half expected to be refused, and was agreeably surprised when the clerk said that the chief would see him.

He found the merchant seated in a swivel-chair, smoking a cigar, while he sorted a number of bills which lay on the desk before him. He gave his visitor a careless nod over his shoulder, but went on with his work for fully ten minutes, without taking any notice of him. Ingomar, who was yet standing in the middle of the floor, was on the point of beating a retreat, when the consul suddenly wheeled about in his chair and faced him.

" Well, young man, what can I do for you?" he asked abruptly.

Ingomar had a good mind to answer in the same tone that he could do nothing for him; but his promise to Ragna, and the great interest he had at stake restrained him.

" I have made an invention, Mr. Consul," he said, " but I cannot test its worth until I can have my model reproduced in steel. This would cost upward of two hundred dollars, and I have come to you to ask you if you would lend me the money, and take your security in the patent which I shall procure, as soon as I have made my test."

Prebensen pinched his small, shrewd eyes together, and looked at the youth as a fox looks at a chicken of which he expects to make a meal. What a contrast they presented, — the one so tall and handsome, with a face so guileless and open and eyes so frank and blue; the other small and wizened, with slyness, deceit, and greed stamped upon his features! It was impossible to imagine a noble emotion in a man with a face like that.

Prebensen did not immediately reply, when Ingomar had explained his errand. He knew the whole story from Ragna, who had labored with him for a full hour to extort from him a promise to help the young inventor; but he enjoyed seeing Vang's son stand before him as a petitioner, and he could not deny himself the pleasure of humiliating him by making him feel his power.

" H'm ! " he muttered at last. " You are a sort of — genius, I suppose. Is that it? "

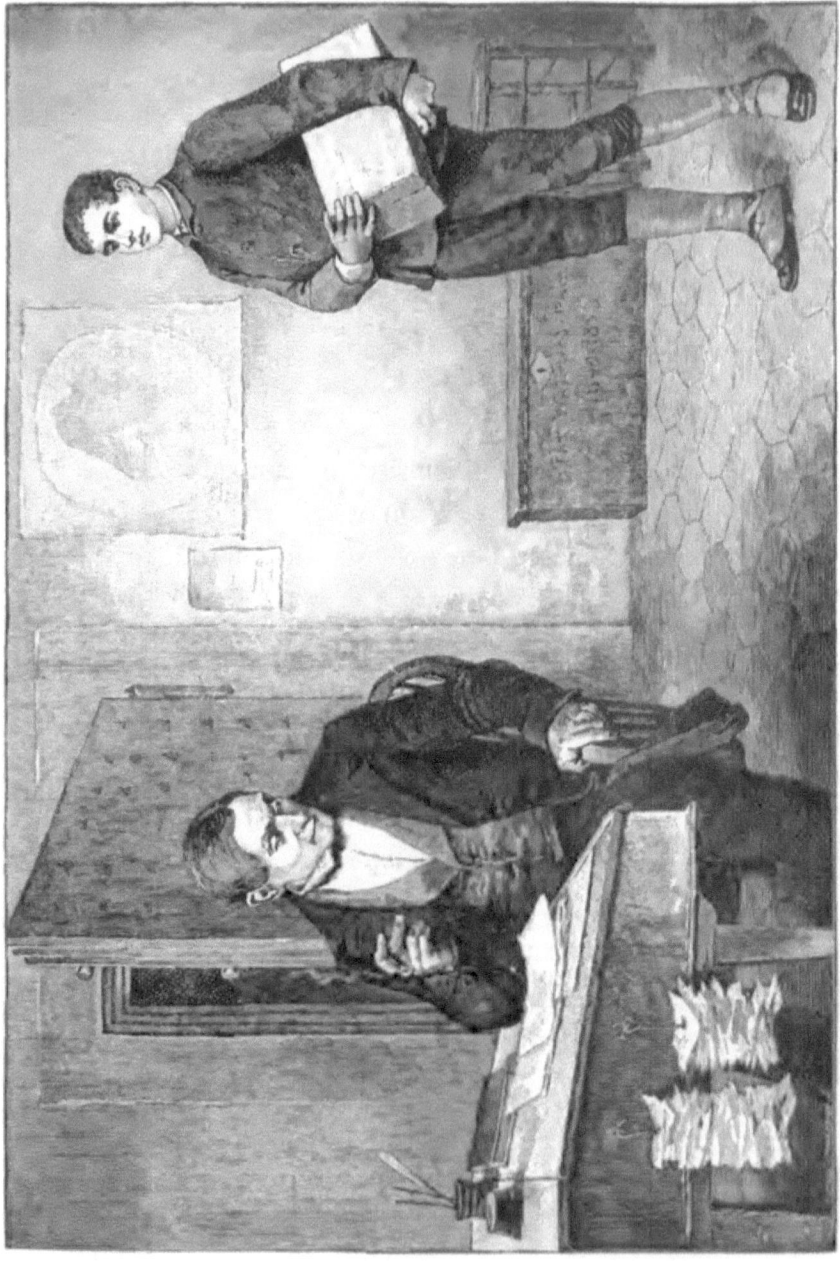

" I have n't said that, Mr. Consul," replied Ingomar, blushing. "I have only said I have made an invention."

" Well, well, it amounts to the same thing, I fancy. If you had n't been a genius, you would n't have made the invention, — that is, of course, if your invention amounts to anything."

"I think it does, sir. In fact, I am sure it does."

" Exactly, there we have it. It amounts to the same thing. But before investing in your genius, I shall have to know more about it. Will you please explain to me the character of your invention? I am not a man to buy the cat in the bag, you know."

Ingomar with alacrity opened his box and placed the swivel-gun on the desk. It was very skilfully made, finished with exquisite neatness, and ornamented with carvings in low relief representing scenes from the life of the whaler.

" Did you make this?" queried the consul, evidently admiring the workmanship.

" Yes, sir, I made it."

" And now let us hear how it works."

The inventor took the gun and unscrewed it into four separate pieces. His features lighted up with happy pride as he began to explain the principle of construction; and the animation of his features, as he told of his various experiments and failures, was touching. If Prebensen had possessed a particle of sentiment, he would have been moved by the boy's enthusiasm; but Prebensen's one thought was not of the boy, but of himself.

He was determined to possess himself of the secret, and, in case it was worth anything, to deprive the inventor of the fruits of his labor. He listened with an almost anxious intentness, and made Ingomar repeat each difficult statement, until he felt sure he understood it.

He saw at a glance that such a gun, if it accomplished what Ingomar claimed, would revolutionize the whaling business. It would enable the ships to hunt right at the coast for the leaner Finmark whale, instead of

going on long and dangerous voyages after
the larger and fatter Greenland whale. It
would nearly double the catch, and would
give a reasonable guarantee of profits, while
greatly lessening the expense. He saw al·
ready in spirit the wealth and power it would
bring him if once it were his; and to make
sure that nothing should escape him of the
details, he took out his notebook and jotted
down some memoranda.

While Ingomar was glowing with delight
at the interest the consul took in his invention, and already confident of receiving the
loan, he was suddenly struck by the peculiar
expression in Prebensen's face. He had
never seen such an expression in any human
face before. It was a kind of wolfish smile,
— the joy of a beast of prey when its
victim approaches within the range of its
clutches.

Ingomar paused for a moment in his ex-
planation, and wiped his forehead with his
handkerchief. He began to grow uneasy.

That strange, greedy smile set him thinking. Could it be possible that Prebensen

was knave enough to steal his invention?
This innocent boy had never come in contact with human depravity, and could
scarcely persuade himself that such wicked-
ness could invade a human heart. Nevertheless, it would do no harm to be cautious.
He resolved quickly not to divulge the com-
position of his bombs, and without the bombs
the gun would be useless.

When he had finished, Prebensen looked
over his memoranda, and glancing up, asked
eagerly, —

" But those bombs in the harpoon? You
did n't tell me what they are made of."

" Excuse me, Consul, but that is my secret," the boy replied, with a reserve which
contrasted with his former enthusiasm. " I
can only assure you that they will accomplish all I claim for them. I'll allow you
to test them yourself, as soon as I get my
steel model."

The consul gave a start and turned pale.
He had not expected that reply. He had
felt sure that the guileless boy would give
himself entirely into his power.

" How can you expect me to stake money
on your invention when you won't explain
it to me?" he asked, with forced gentleness.
Inwardly he was growling, and longing to
strike his claws into this impudent youth
who dared to balk him.

" I think I have explained enough to show
you that you may stake your money with
safety," Ingomar replied.

" Beware, young man, I give you fair
warning! If you want me to help you, you
must n't hold anything back."

" I have said enough to give you a guar-
anty of good faith."

" How do I know but that you have been
lying to me all the while?"

"I never lied in all my life," cried Ingomar, proudly; "and you, Consul Prebensen,
are shrewd enough to know that what I have
told you is the truth!"

" Then out with it, out with it, I tell you!
Speak out now, and be quick about it! You
shall have the money if you tell me all, but
otherwise not a cent. Or no, hold on! You
might invent something to stuff me, know-

ing that I am not a scientist. But anyway,
I 'll risk it. Speak out, and the money is
yours."

But Ingomar could not speak. He was
firmly convinced now that Prebensen would
in some way outwit him. So he calmly
screwed the pieces together, deposited the
gun in the box, and seizing his hat backed
toward the door.

"You 'll repent of your folly some day!"
snarled the consul after him. "I 'll make
you repent of it, you fool! How dare you
come here and insult me in my own
house?"

He started up threateningly; but Ingomar
met his eye unflinchingly, and in no wise
hastened his movements. With perfect com-
posure he walked out through the store,
though his blood was hot with anger and
disappointment. The glare of the sunshine
made his eyes ache, and his temples
throbbed.

And so, adieu, fond dream! How was he
now to make his invention useful? And all
the anxious days and the sleepless nights

he had spent, tossed between hope and fear, were now wasted, nay, worse than wasted.

With these sad reflections he sauntered along, scarcely feeling the touch of the earth beneath his feet. He had got about half-way down the hill, not far from the invisible wire, when he spied Sophus Prebensen, the consul's son, picking his way daintily over the pavement. He wore a new silk hat, a light brown summer overcoat, and new light trousers of a stylish pattern.

He was, as usual, smoking a cigarette, and flourishing a silver-handled bamboo walking-stick in his hand. Quite unsuspicious of the trap that lay in his path, he came striding along, with his nose in the air, when lo! the invisible wire knocked off his new hat, and sent it dancing into the gutter.

Sophus stopped, picked up his beaver with great deliberation, and stared vindictively up and down the street. Stealthily he approached the corner behind which he knew the plotters must be concealed; and when one unwary urchin put his head forward to

see if the coast was clear, Sophus grabbed
him by the hair and began to beat him
mercilessly with his stick.

The boy yelled at the top of his voice, as
well he might, for the stout cane came whiz-
zing through the air, whack, whack, whack,
and was raising tremendous welts on his
back.

Ingomar had stopped at the first scream
of the boy, but had not felt called upon to
interfere, as long as he believed the lad was
only receiving a reasonable punishment; but
when he heard his heart-rending shrieks and
saw the fury in his assailant's face, his generous wrath got the better of him, and he
bounded forward, seized Sophus by the arm,
and cried, —

"Are n't you ashamed of yourself to be
beating a little fellow like that?"

The bully, thus suddenly arrested, wheeled
about and glared savagely at Ingomar.
"What business is it of yours, anyway?"
he asked.

"If anybody behaves like a brute to a
defenceless little chap, it *is* my business, and

if it is n't, I 'll *make* it my business," Ingomar replied.

"It was n't me did it!" croaked the little gamin, rising with difficulty, but tumbling again into the gutter. "It was Bernt Olsen."

His rescuer stooped down over him to see if he was much hurt, and discovered that it was Tobias's son Tom. He had just put his hand on the lad's shoulder, and was about to lift him up, when he heard the cane whiz about his ears, and felt a stinging pain across his back.

"I 'll teach you to meddle with what does n't concern you!" were the words which accompanied the blow.

Ingomar darted up like a rocket, snatched the cane out of his opponent's hand, and flourished it about his head.

"You know I can whip you into flinders," he cried, forcibly restraining his anger; "but I 'll have pity on you, and only give you back what I owe you!" and raising the cane, he gave Sophus a smart blow across his calves, and hurled the stick into the gutter.

The bully, receiving now a taste of what he had inflicted upon little Tom, grew livid with rage. He flung himself against Ingomar, beat blindly about him, scratched, bit, and kicked; but two or three blows which made the sparks dance before his eyes soon reduced him to submission. With a swollen nose, a crushed hat, and a much demoralized toilet, the young dandy continued his way, almost crying with pain and vowing dire vengeance.

Ingomar picked up little Tom and carried him home.

CHAPTER V.

A BLOW IN THE DARK.

INGOMAR felt sure, after his encounter with Sophus, that Prebensen was meditating revenge upon him, for Sophus was the apple of his eye. Even if he might be willing to forgive Ingomar's distrust of him in refusing to part with his invention, he would never forgive the black eye given to his son and heir.

Ingomar tried to guess what form the consul's revenge might take, but he could not guess anything that seemed at all likely. A square and open attack of whatever nature he would not have feared; but it was Prebensen's way to strike in the dark, and against a blow in the dark no one can defend himself.

There was, however, one thing which interested him more than anything he had to fear from Prebensen, and that was the testing

and perfecting of his invention. There was
but one way left by which he might hope in
time to save up the money needed for the
steel model; but that was such a slow way
that he had not thought of resorting to it,
until he knew that it was the only way left.

There was a good demand for mounted
birds. By stuffing fine specimens of gulls
and auks and penguins, and selling them to
the tourists, he might in two years become a
capitalist to the extent of two hundred dollars; but two years seemed an eternity to
the impatient boy, burning with eagerness to
see his daring dream realized. However, as
there was now no help for it, a slow way
was surely better than no way.

The third day after his interview with the
consul, Ingomar called on Tobias, and asked
him to accompany him for a day's hunt
to the Twin Islands. The mate, who was
anxious to get on friendly terms again with
his favorite, was nothing loath; and off they
started together in Vang's sail-boat, the
"Black Swan."

The wind, which was from the southwest,

filled the sail as they tacked out of the harbor, and promised to keep steady, at least until the afternoon. They had a rifle and a fowling-piece wrapped in oilskin cases in the bottom of the boat, and a luncheon-basket containing bread, butter, smoked ham, and a bottle of milk. A keg of fresh water, an extra suit of oil-clothes for each of them, and a couple of boat-hooks completed their equipment.

Tobias was in brave spirits, and told stories about his adventures on the high seas. Sitting astride the rear thwart, smoking a clay-pipe, he scanned the horizon, which stretched bright and blue toward the ice-bound pole.

" I tell ye, lad," he said, blowing the blue smoke lazily into the air, " them was great times when I sailed as cabin-boy in the 'Polar Star.' Mighty cantankerous craft that 'Polar Star' was; a bit too broad in her beam to be a first-class racer, but sound in her j'ints; and she could carry more sail fur her size than any ship I ever clapped eyes on. She made no end of money fur yer dad on her first voyages; and it was on her

very first voyage that I had the fattest job I
ever had in my life."

"How was that, Tobias?"

"How it was? Wal, lad, it was fat, I tell
ye; that's what it was. Ye know the sperm-
whale? Wal, he ain't anywhere near so big
as the Greenland whale; and one day when
we had harpooned one of them little chaps,
his head, which was full of sperm ile, had
been cut off and h'isted aboard. As I was
a-sayin', I was only cabin-boy in them days,
and I suspicion I was a bit green; anyway,
as I came running up from below to see what
the racket was, the head of the whale which
the lads had cut open caught my eye, and
I rushed up to it.

"'Toby,' cries Anders Nelson, the second
mate, — he was a bit of a wag, he was, —
'the cap'n has dropped his gold watch
into that whale's head, and he offers a dollar
to any man as can fish it out.'

"He didn't have to tell me that twice. I
plunged my arm up to the shoulder-j'int into
the sperm ile; but in the same moment my
feet slipped in the grease, and I tumbled

head-foremost into the whale's skull. There
I lay flounderin' and splutterin', for I
could n't get no footin' anywhere; and the
lads, they roared and yelled and shrieked,
and nearly killed themselves larfin'."

"But how did you get out, Tobias?"

"How did I get out? Wal, I should n't
never have got out, if Anders Nelson, the
second mate, seein' the joke had gone far
enough, had n't pulled me out by the legs,
and flung me on a coil of rope; and there I
sat, as sick as a dog, snortin' and gaspin';
and the ile ran down my face from my hair,
jest as it did in the times of Aaron, only I
had n't no beard then, like as Aaron had.
But anyway, lad, there ain't no denyin' that
that was the fattest job I ever had."

When they were well out of the harbor,
the wind veered about and struck them
abeam. The long, smooth ocean swell, as it
lifted the "Black Swan" and let her slide
again into the hollows, produced a rocking
motion which would have been trying to a
land-lubber. The sun was dazzlingly bright,
the sky cloudless, and the sea seemed a

great expanse of myriad shining dimples.
All the time whales were spouting and
blowing columns of spray high into the air;
but Tobias steered carefully out of the way
of those monsters, as it was not safe to encounter them in an open boat.

Now and then a family of seals raised their
glossy heads out of the water, and vanished
with a splash before Ingomar could get shot
at them. As they neared the Twin Islands,
they caught sight of another sail-boat that
seemed to be heading for the same point.
They signalled to her two or three times, but
she did not answer.

" Whose boat is that, Tobias?" asked
Ingomar.

" She looks to me like Prebensen's ' Penguin,' " answered the mate.

"What is she doing so far from shore, I
wonder?" the boy observed with a lively
interest. " Neither the consul nor Sophus is
much for sport. I don't believe they know
how to handle a gun, either of them."

" No, nor could they sail a boat like that.
But the lass, though, she can handle the sail

with one hand, and the tiller with the other. I 've seen her do it."

" So have I. But what could she be doing out here? "

Tobias smoked for some minutes in silence; then he shook his head and observed, " ' No one knows where the hare goes,' said the man, when he put his trap on the roof."

He sat watching the strange boat with a mystified air, and Ingomar saw that there was something that puzzled him.

" Pretty reckless sailing that! " he remarked, as the " Penguin " rounded the point of the island. " Look how she runs up into the wind! "

The Twin Islands, which rise out of the Arctic Ocean, are two enormous rocks that rest on a common foundation, split in two, as it were, by the raging surf, which beats forever with a thundering roar against their base. The one known as the Reindeer Island has some scant vegetation on the sheltered side, particularly reindeer moss, and a kind of delicious berries called *multer*,

which are so much liked that people travel
long distances to taste them

The Horn Island — for so the other twin is
named — points two black, threatening crags
against the sky, and is the home of thousands
of birds, which cover every inch of the rock
on the seaward side.

There the great auks and the puffins sit in
long regular rows, like soldiers on parade,
looking as grave as judges. The gulls fight
for dear life to gain possession of an exposed
ledge of the cliff upon which petrels and surf-
scoters have encroached. The black cormorants, those feathered thieves, sit calmly
watching the sea, and whenever a gull or an
auk has caught a fish, they pounce upon her,
and with angry screams and blows tear the
booty out of her bill; nay, if she has swal-
lowed it, they often compel her to gulp it up
again.

At the base of the crags the eider-ducks
have their nests; and for miles the sea is
thickly covered with their downy brood, taking their first swimming-lessons. They are
so tame that they scarcely move out of the

way if you try to catch them. They seem
to be aware that the law protects them, and
that there is a fine imposed upon him who
does them harm.

Between the two crags which the birds
occupy there is a natural entrance, like a
portal, into the interior of the island. Here,
you would suppose, in this wide, sheltered
space, Nature had provided a most desir-
able and delightful breeding-place for the
feathered hosts that make their living out
of the sea.

But, strange to say, not a bird is to be
seen. The bare, black rocks do not support
a single nest. While a desperate fight is
going on for every inch of the exposed crag
on the seaward side, and blood is shed and
the heavens are filled with the noise of
the combat, here neither gull nor auk nor
cormorant seeks a refuge, and the tumult
of wing-beats and screams is dimly heard
through the roar of the surf, softened by the
distance.

It is, of course, no art to kill a hundred
birds or more where the multitude is so great

that every shot fired at random must bring
down a dozen. The first shot Ingomar fired
produced such an ear-splitting din that he
was loath to fire another. It was as if he
had conjured up a snow-storm of white-
winged living and screaming things.

He had picked out a beautiful specimen of
a great auk, which by means of the boat-hook
he fished out of the surf. A second and a
third shot brought down a royal penguin and
a burgomaster gull, which, on account of
their size and rarity, are much prized by
collectors.

He had managed to land in a little sheltered cove on the southwestern side of the
island, but finding no safe anchorage, had
left Tobias in the boat. Having killed as
many birds as he needed to stuff, he began
to climb the slippery rocks, the ledges of
which were so densely covered with nests
that he could scarcely move without treading
on eggs or hatching birds.

It seemed to him all of a sudden that he
heard through the screams of the gulls a
human voice calling his name. He sup-

posed at first that he must be dreaming, for
it was not the voice of Tobias, and moreover
Tobias was cruising about the island with a
trolling-line, wishing to utilize the time until
his master should wish to return.

Ingomar seated himself on a ledge of the
rock and listened.

Yes, there could be no doubt of it. Some
one was calling him. Before answering he
climbed around the crag to a place where he
had a view of the cove, and there, to his
amazement, he saw the " Penguin," and
Ragna standing in the prow with a rope in
her hand.

" Look out! " he shouted. " You can't
anchor there! "

Leaping with the aid of the boat-hook
from rock to rock, he made a tremendous
commotion among the birds, but reached in
a few minutes the cove.

" Here," she cried, " catch the rope! "

" But you can't land here," he was about
to answer; but before he could utter the
words he had the rope about his neck, and
had no choice but to haul her in. He would

have protested once more, when Ragna put her hands on his shoulders and leaped out upon the stones.

But he knew that when Ragna made up her mind to do a thing, it was of no use to protest against it. He therefore waded out into the water and anchored the " Penguin " as safely as the circumstances permitted.

" But tell me now," he began, when he stood, dripping and wet, at her side, "what does this mean?"

" I can't hear my own voice here," she shouted; " those birds make such an awful racket! Let us go in through this gate; perhaps it is quieter inside."

He followed her wonderingly through the rocky portal. The wind blew her yellow hair about her face, and her eyes shone with excitement.

" Ingomar," she said, as soon as the noise subsided, " I want you to go away from here."

" Go away from where? " he queried in astonishment.

" From Vardöe, — from your home."

" But why — why should I go away?"

" Do you remember what you once said to me? You said you were going to be a great man. Here at home you will never be anything but what you are now."

" You wait and see."

They were now within the great rocky hall. The black walls rose on all sides with their jagged outline against the sky; the floor, though uneven, was rather smooth, as if worn in past ages by the action of the waves. There was a muffled roar in the air as of a mighty wind far away, but they could talk easily without raising their voices.

The girl paused for a moment, and stared as if startled at the wild and lonesome aspect of the place. Then she seated herself on a bowlder, while Ingomar flung the birds he had shot on the ground, and placed himself in front of her, leaning upon his gun.

There was something almost imploring in the way she glanced up into his face; and the thought flashed through his brain that she must have some very weighty reason for wishing him to leave home, since she had come so far to give him the warning.

"Don't beat about the bush, Ragna," he said, returning her earnest look. "You have some other reason for wishing me to go."

"Well, what if I have?" she answered resolutely. She blushed, however, in spite of herself, and looked away in confusion. "I wish you had n't hurt Sophus," she murmured, struggling with her tears; "it is that which has made all the mischief, and what makes me so miserable is that it was I who brought it all on you."

"You? How so?"

"I advised you to see father about your invention, and he promised me to lend you the money, if you could satisfy him that it was worth anything; and I was so happy about it!"

"Well, but you see I did n't satisfy him."

"Oh, I don't understand it at all!" cried the girl, giving free vent to her grief; "but if you had n't gone to see father, you would n't have met Sophus, and I should n't be so unhappy as I am."

"Then it is on your father's account you want me to leave?"

She bowed her head, covered her face with her hands, and wept piteously. "I only tell you this, — that you must go, Ingomar," she pleaded.

"Then tell me why."

"Well — well — " She raised her head, and wiped away her tears with her handkerchief; "but why must you compel me to say it?"

"Because I must know it. Otherwise I shall not go."

"Well — my father — he hates you, Ingomar. I know — both he and Sophus — mean to do you harm."

"And is that the reason you came to see me here?"

"Yes; I couldn't see you in town."

"How do they mean to harm me?"

"That I don't know, for they don't quite trust me. But it is so hard, Ingomar, to hear them talk of you as they do. You have always been so good to me, and I can't bear to hear any one speak ill of you."

She looked up at him with a sweet, tearful smile, which was so appealing that he could not help smiling in return, though he was anything but joyous.

" Ragna," he said, " I should like to follow your advice, but I cannot. I love this place, I have spent all my life here; and if it comes to that, — no one can drive me away, I am not afraid of anybody."

" Oh, you don't know what you are saying!" she cried. " You are a boy — and my father — oh, you don't know him! He is very rich and very — powerful! "

She continued to plead with him for a long while, appealing now to his ambition and the brilliant chances of success which the great world offered him, if he would but reach out his hand and seize them. To him departure at this time appeared like flight from an enemy; and against such an appearance his manly pride rebelled.

Seeing that she could accomplish nothing by her entreaties, Ragna took her leave; and he helped her into the boat, pulled up the anchor for her, and stood knee-deep in the water, watching with admiration her clever seamanship.

How prompt, how agile and deft she was in all her turns and movements! Now she ran up the sail just at the right moment, turned the tiller, and scudded away over the sea, through the swarms of screaming birds, and was soon out of sight.

Ingomar fired a shot as a signal to Tobias to lay to. He was so much stirred by what he had heard that he had lost all taste for further sport. They ate their luncheon in silence, and after some more trolling for cod, turned the prow homeward. But as ill luck would have it, the wind fell off, and for more than four hours the sail hung slack and they made no headway against the tide, which was running out.

The sun lost its brightness as it sank toward the sea, and grew fiery red. A purplish mist hovered along the horizon; and the Twin Isles, as they lifted their frowning brows above the ocean, looked as if they had been steeped in blood. Gradually the flaming splendor spread over the whole sky, and land and water swam in a crimson glow.

As the night approached, the colors grew deeper and more wildly intense; and strange it was to see the screaming swarm of birds, deluded by the light, dive, swim, and fly with the rosy flush of the midnight sun upon their wings.

It was not until the last bit of provisions in the basket had been eaten that the sail of the "Black Swan" began to flap and then suddenly bulged out. You could see the wind approaching like a track of flame across the waters; and it was hailed with shouts of joy, after the long and tedious drifting.

It was about one o'clock in the morning when they reached Vardöe; and it was none too soon, for the wind had increased to a storm, the sky had darkened, and the sun had vanished behind a black veil of cloud.

Wearily they' trudged up through the deserted streets, Tobias carrying the killed birds, and Ingomar the rifles and hunting-gear. At Mr. Vang's front door they separated, with a promise to meet on the morrow, for the tourist season was now at its height. If any money was to be realized from the birds, they would have to be stuffed and mounted at once; and for the rougher part of this work the aid of Tobias was almost indispensable.

Not wishing to arouse his father, who was a poor sleeper, Ingomar determined to spend the night in his workshop, where he had a sofa and some pillows; for as he had expected to be home at a much earlier hour, he had not thought of taking a latch-key.

Picking up his birds, which were very heavy, he crossed the court-yard, entered the stable, and fumbled his way up the stairs.

It seemed to him suddenly that he saw a flash of light through the key-hole, and heard the creaking of boots and the tread of wary footsteps. What could it be? His heart stood still, and his breath stuck in his throat.

There could be no doubt of it! There was some one above in his workshop. The light had been quickly blown out, but he could hear a faint sound as of hands groping for the door. Ingomar pressed himself

tightly against the wall, and stood still as
a mouse. Whoever the intruder was, he
should not escape him.

Ragna's warning occurred to him, and for a
moment his blood ran cold. But who would
have expected to find him here at this hour?
No, it was not to do him bodily harm that
this nocturnal visitor was abroad. He could
scarcely guess any other purpose, and he was
too excited, for the moment, to be ingenious
at guessing.

For five, ten, nay, fifteen minutes he stood
there in the dark, pressed up against the
wall. He began to grow impatient. Was it
likely that the intruder could have escaped
through the window? That, to be sure, was
not improbable.

The boy felt himself growing hot at the
thought of such a possibility. He could en-
dure his uncertainty no longer. He took
one, two, three steps; and the rickety old
stairs creaked horribly under his weight.

He was within two steps of the top, when
suddenly the door was torn open, and a
figure dashed plumb against him, knocked

him over, so that he tumbled down the whole length of the stairs, and then darted out of sight across the court-yard and into the street.

By the time Ingomar had picked himself up, it would have been hopeless to look for the fugitive. A fine, drizzling rain was falling, and it was quite dusky. There were a hundred hiding-places in the sea-booths and rigging-lofts, and among the innumerable barrels that were piled about the wharves.

Ingomar stood for some minutes in the stable-door and gazed out into the twilight. His shoulder, which was badly bruised, pained him, and he had a big bump on his forehead, which had been struck in the fall.

But it was not this which occupied his thought. Who could this midnight visitor have been, and what could have been his object in breaking into the workshop? An ordinary thief would have known better than to break in where there was nothing to steal.

And there was nothing in that shop which

would be of value to anybody — except — except — the harpoon gun !

Ingomar turned about and darted up the stairs like a shot. He felt dizzy. The blood throbbed in his ears. The harpoon gun, — his invention, the child of his sorrow, which he loved above all other things, upon which he had expended his best thought and energy, about which revolved his ambition and his hopes of success ! Reeling across the floor like a drunken man, he fumbled above the chimney for the match-safe, struck a light, and rushed with a wild fear in his eyes toward the turning-bench.

The match went out, and with tremulous hands he struck another. He took his time now, lighted a candle, and stood for a while staring into the flame, bracing himself as for a blow.

He could doubt no longer; and as he slowly turned about, he was prepared for what he saw. The harpoon gun was gone ! The drawer of the table where he kept his chemical formulæ and the results of his

experiments had been broken open, and
every bit of paper it contained had been
carried away.

The thief had worked at his leisure, evidently believing he was safe from interruption, and had made thorough work of it.

Ingomar stood pale and still, with the
candle in his hands, gazing at the ruin of his
hopes. He scarcely dared to think.

It was all over with him. His invention,
upon which he had staked his all, was in the
hands of another, and in the hands of one
who would not hesitate to realize whatever
profit there was in it. For though he had
had no glimpse of the thief, he knew as well
as if he had seen him that it was either Prebensen or some one whom he had employed.

He could have wept; but his grief was too
bitter for tears. A burning indignation, a
consuming wrath, took possession of him.
He had hoped to forge a weapon by means
of which his father should again rise to his
former position and the family recover its
lost eminence; and now that weapon was
actually in his enemy's hand, and would be

8

used to crush and utterly annihilate his father.

While these bitter reflections filled his mind, Ingomar's glance fell by chance upon the little shelf above the chimney.

Suddenly his face brightened. His eyes dilated with a new hope. To ward off the shock of another disappointment, he advanced slowly, cautiously; put his hand on a little box on the shelf, and took it down.

Panting with emotion, he stood gazing at the little black and coppery-red balls it contained. They were bombs, — half-a-dozen in all, — the only ones he had made.

He remembered now having taken them out of the drawer the day before, and neglected to put them back; and by this accident he had saved his secret. By being left with no effort at concealment, they had escaped the attention of the thief.

The only thing Prebensen had secured which might enable him to solve the riddle was the papers recording the results of the chemical experiments. If he possessed the knowledge to read them, he might learn how to make the bombs. But this knowledge Ingomar knew Prebensen did not possess.

There was, however, yet a possibility which filled Ingomar with apprehension. The consul might easily call to his aid some one who could decipher the chemical riddle, and so discover his secret.

CHAPTER VI.

A FRIEND IN NEED.

INGOMAR was clever enough to realize that he had no time to lose. It was now a race between Prebensen and him as to who should first procure the patent.

That the consul had sent the papers and the model to some famous scientist, — or at least the papers, for he was too shrewd to reveal more than a part of his secret to any one man, — Ingomar knew as well as if he had read the letter containing the instructions.

His first thought had been to report the whole affair to the police, and prosecute the thief; but his father dissuaded him so earnestly from taking this course that he had to abandon it. Prebensen was too powerful a man to be captured in that way. He had a hundred resources where Ingomar had but one, and in so desperate a combat the weaker would be not only ruined, but utterly crushed.

Thus matters stood when, one fine morning, an English pleasure-yacht came steaming up the Busse Sound, and dropped her anchor in the harbor. Ingomar, who had been at work during the last week on a new model of his harpoon gun, containing some improvements, besides in his leisure moments stuffing and preparing sea-birds, levelled his telescope at the fine ship, and read on the prow the name " Lady Jane Gray."

He saw here an opportunity to earn some money, and accordingly lost no time in rowing out to the yacht with his stuffed birds.

The proprietor, Sir Robert Graham, a wealthy iron-master from Manchester, received him kindly, and bought his burgomaster gull and the great auk for three pounds.

The baronet, who was a tall, burly man, with a bushy, iron-gray beard, apparently took a fancy to the handsome youth, introduced him to Lady Graham and the other members of the party, and conversed with

him about the sports and the industries of
the island. He engaged Ingomar as his
guide and cicerone during the three or four
days he intended to spend in the neighborhood, and by his kindness and consideration
soon gained his confidence.

"Mr. Vang," he said one evening, as they
sat on deck gazing at the flaming midnight
sun, "I suppose, like other youths, you have
your ambition. Tell me, my lad, what do
you intend to make of yourself?"

Ingomar hesitated before answering, and
the thought darted through his brain that
here was the man who could help him, if
he would. "I intend to be an inventor,"
he replied boldly.

"An inventor, oho! Is n't that rather a
curious trade?" queried Sir Robert, with a
laugh.

"Perhaps; but, with your permission, sir,
that is what I am, and I doubt if I shall
amount to anything if I try to be anything
else."

"Aha! Why, that is interesting! Perhaps you have invented something already?"

" Yes, I have."

" Would it be indiscreet to ask what it is?"

Ingomar's head was in a whirl. Suddenly, like a tempting will-o'-the-wisp, hope danced once more before his eyes. He considered rapidly the consequences of confiding in a stranger; but feeling sure that this stranger was a good and honorable man, he quickly decided to take the risk.

" I have invented a harpoon gun for catching whale," he said, flushing with eager excitement; " but a thief came in the night and stole my model."

" Stole your model?" ejaculated Sir Robert and Lady Graham in the same breath. " And has the thief taken out a patent?"

" Not yet, but he will unless I get the better of him."

At the iron-master's request Ingomar now told the story of his experiments, explained the principle of his gun, and, as his agitation rose, fairly amazed his auditors by his eloquence. It was touching to see how his face lighted up with pleasure as he described all the blessings to the district and to all Norway that would flow from the new order of things which would result from his invention.

He spoke in a simple and straightforward way, and yet with a warmth and spirit which made a deep impression upon Sir Robert and Lady Graham. Sir Robert, who was himself a manufacturer of machinery, saw at once that there was something practical in the boy's idea; and the questions he asked showed Ingomar that here was one at least who fully understood him.

When he had finished his narrative, the Englishman sat for a while smoking in silence. Ingomar looked anxiously at him. It seemed to him as if his whole future was trembling in the balance.

" The Bible says that ' the way of transgressors is hard,' " observed Lady Graham, " but I should say that the way of the inventor is even harder."

" Yes, it is a thorny path, — the path of the inventor. It has always been so," answered the baronet. " I would advise you to try something else, young man," he continued, addressing Ingomar. "Without large means or powerful protection you'll never make a success of your invention."

He eyed the young man sharply while he spoke, as if he would read his very soul. The poor fellow, seeing his hope again vanish, felt as if the ground had suddenly given way under his feet. He felt dizzy; and his heart, though it kept thumping violently against his side, was like a lump of lead in his breast.

His first impulse was to turn his back on Sir Robert, and show him the contempt he felt for him; for how could he doubt that he too, having abundant means at his command, intended to steal his invention? He was an unlucky fellow, indeed, destined to be betrayed by every one whom he trusted.

His pride, however, came to his rescue. He would not give Sir Robert the satisfaction of seeing how deeply he was wounded. So, repressing every sign of emotion, he turned a pale, resolute face toward the baronet, and said, "I am sorry to have troubled you with my affairs, sir. I shall not presume to do so again."

"And then you 'll give it up, won't you, and take up some more useful calling?" urged Sir Robert, smiling at the boy's haughty manner.

"No, sir, I shall never give it up!" Ingomar replied hotly. "As long as there is a drop of blood left in me I shall fight; and if I fall, I shall fall fighting."

"Bravo, young man, bravo!" cried Sir Robert, jumping up and grasping his hand. "You 've the right stuff in you, I see that. I only wanted to test you. I believe in your invention, and you shall not have trusted in me in vain. I will cheerfully bear the expense of putting your model in steel, and you can pay me back when your patent begins to be profitable."

"Oh, thank you, sir, thank you!"

If the sky had tumbled down about his ears, the young inventor could not have been more astonished. He scarcely dared to trust his own ears. The deck seemed to billow under his feet, and the fiery mists that draped the horizon gave an air of strange, almost magic unreality to everything that came within the range of his eyes.

Perhaps he was only dreaming, and would wake up presently and find the barren, cruel reality confronting him. He stared at Sir Robert and Lady Graham with a desperate determination to hold them fast, and to prevent them from vanishing into golden vapors; and the great burly voice of the baronet, when it spoke out again in tones of encouragement, was to Ingomar's ears the sweetest music to which he had ever listened.

"How would you like going back with us to England?" he asked. "I have a big machine-shop in Manchester, where I employ upward of two thousand men. There you can work out your idea at your leisure; and when you have made your final tests, you can patent the gun both in England and Norway. That would more than double your profits."

It is not necessary to record the discussion that followed. The end of it was that Ingomar, with his father's consent, sailed for

England with Sir Robert Graham. There he labored for a year with unwearied diligence in Sir Robert's machine-shop, and became in an extraordinarily short time an expert machinist. The day when he had finished his model in steel his happiness knew no bounds.

In the evening he was invited to dine at Sir Robert's house, and was treated with such consideration by every one present that his bashfulness quite vanished. He was beguiled by Lady Graham into talking about his native land, and describing the Twin Islands and the great breeding colonies of the Arctic birds. Ingomar did not think he had ever spent so pleasant an evening in all his life.

"I suppose," said Sir Robert, when the guests had departed, "that what we now have to do is to take out your patent, and the next thing will be to test the gun."

"Sir Robert," Ingomar answered, "I want to confer upon you my patent rights for England in return for what you have done for me. I am now sure the thing will work, but without you I should never have been sure of anything."

"And there is another thing that has occurred to me in this connection," he went on to say. "If you can make sure that the dead whale will float, there is no need of fitting up sailing vessels for long voyages. A small, strong, steel-armored steamer will then be much more serviceable. There are plenty of Finmark whale along the Arctic coasts of Norway; and my idea is that the steamer, as soon as a whale has been killed, should tow it ashore, cut off the blubber and the whalebone there, and convert the meat into fertilizers. Then nothing will be wasted.

"A small steamer of twenty-horse power could hunt the whale on a grand scale. It could race with him, tire him out, shoot the harpoon into his belly, and tow him ashore. If my gun is to be a perfect success, I must make or hire a small steamer for our first expedition."

The young man who spoke thus had gotten larger ideas of life since he left Norway.

He formed daring plans now, and saw already the golden fruit of success dangling before his eager vision.

But, to do him justice, it was not the gold that excited his fancy. He had a noble and generous nature. His first desire was to restore his father to the position of which he had, by foul means, been deprived; and secondly, to help the poor and miserable people of his native town by offering them steady work, at wages which would enable them to spend their lives in tolerable comfort.

The idea of hunting whale with steam and artillery delighted Sir Robert. It seemed in harmony with the modern age. The old Norse god of strength, Thor, who fished for the world-serpent with an anchor baited with the head of a bull, became a pygmy compared to this modern monster with the strength of twenty horses, belching forth steam and smoke, shooting the barbed harpoon into the body of its prey, and making the whale explode, by its first effort at escape, a deadly charge of powder, bullets, and volatile gases.

It was all so complex, — so intricate and ingenious. It bore the stamp of a daring spirit. The boy who at so early an age could dream such dreams, even though they should prove to be nothing but dreams, was a genius, and deserved all the encouragement which wealth and cordial sympathy could give him.

" By the shade of Moses, my dear fellow, you have got a first-class, patent-excelsior head-piece on your shoulders ! " was the baronet's exclamation when Ingomar had unfolded his plan for the gigantic marine chase. " But at this point permit me a question. You have never yet told me what your bombs are made of. The only doubt in my mind is this. How can you, by the explosion of one or two bombs, small enough to be hidden in the point of the harpoon, generate enough gas to float the enormous carcass of a whale, if it is disposed to sink ? "

" I am glad you asked me that," Ingomar replied. " In the first place you must take into account that the whale's body is about

of the same specific weight as the sea-water.
It would be its natural disposition, by reason
of its blubber (which is lighter than water),
to float; and a fair proportion of Greenland
whales will float without any artificial aid.
But the number of those which sink con-
stitute, as a rule, the difference between
profit and loss in a whaling-voyage. That
margin I intend to save. The force I need
to supply to buoy up the sinking whale is
not in proportion to its huge size. It is but
that little difference between sinking and
floating I have to supply, in a body which
would under normal circumstances float of
itself; but as I have said, the lean whale,
which falls a little below the average, can,
by the supplying of this small additional
force, be saved, and a probability of loss
be turned into a certainty of profit." [1]

The ardor with which Ingomar spoke,
when any question was raised as to his in-

---

[1] The invention here described has actually been made,
and I could easily reveal the real name of the man who
made it; but I fear he would take me to task for such
an indiscretion.

vention, never failed to arouse a sympathetic interest in Sir Robert, who sat and beamed upon him with a sort of paternal pride.

"You make out a very strong case, my lad," he remarked thoughtfully; "we must talk more about this business, and if it proves to be feasible, I'll take care that the means be not lacking to carry it out."

Sir Robert was as good as his word. As soon as he became convinced that the problem presented no insuperable obstacles, he ordered a small steamer to be built on the Clyde in accordance with Ingomar's design. Though careful to reveal no secrets, he consulted scientific experts regarding many details, without yet having his faith shaken in the daring enterprise.

He went to visit Ingomar every afternoon in his private laboratory, talked with him while he worked, and often brought visitors, to whom he introduced the young inventor as a mechanical genius, — a future Fulton or Stephenson. He did this for the purpose of extending Ingomar's acquaintance among influential men, and preparing the public for the surprise which the harpoon gun and the steam chase would make in the near future.

One day, when the Norseman was standing, black as a chimney-sweep, before his forge, conducting an experiment in explosives, with a view to finding a cheaper substitute for one of the ingredients in his bombs, Sir Robert ushered into the room a young Swede, whom he introduced as Mr. Lindgren, the director of the great machine-shop at Mora.

Mr. Lindgren was a tall, blond man, and would have been handsome if it had not been for the lynx-like and uneasy look in his eyes. He was always trying to evade the glance of the person with whom he was talking.

Sir Robert was an easy-going man, and not inclined to distrust any one; but a vague suspicion invaded his mind when, by chance, he noticed how the young Swede's glance, as it were, pounced upon Ingomar, when his back was turned, and then slid off like a shadow the moment the young Norseman faced him.

But, after all, what could Ingomar have to fear from a Swede travelling for his pleasure, who from a very natural interest desired to inspect the workshops of a colleague in his own line of business? A man with dishonest designs would have come in disguise as an artist or scholar or a mere pleasure-seeker, and would not have avowed his knowledge of and interest in machinery.

Thus reasoned Sir Robert, while Mr. Lindgren conversed with Ingomar about the chemical experiments he was conducting. Again he was at no pains to conceal his knowledge, and the baronet ended by laughing at his suspicions. He determined to say nothing to his *protégé* about his dislike of the Swede; and as, on the following day, he was obliged to go to London, he thought no more of the matter.

Contrary to his expectation he was detained in the metropolis for a whole week by important business; and Mr. Lindgren, who had no other acquaintances in Manchester, had to put up with Ingomar's society as a substitute. At all events, he visited the

laboratory daily, and sat and chatted famil-
iarly by the hour.

At the end of the week, when Sir Robert
returned, he bade his new friend farewell,
and started, as he averred, for Birmingham
and Sheffield.

But no sooner was he gone than Ingomar
received a tremendous eye-opener. Though
he had not exactly liked the Swede, it had
never once occurred to him to suspect him
of any dishonest purpose in visiting him.
Such visits are frequent in all large factories;
and where all improvements are protected
by patents, they are expected and even
encouraged.

But the day after Lindgren's departure
Ingomar received two letters from Norway
which set him thinking. The one was anony-
mous, but could have been written by no
one but Ragna Prebensen. It read as
follows : —

"Don't have anything to do with a Swede
named Engström, and don't show him any of
your inventions. This is written by one who
wishes you well."

The other letter, which had obviously cost its author both labor and sorrow, was as difficult to read as it had been to compose. As far as Ingomar could make out, these were its contents: —

Too the wel-born and hyli-respekted masheenist, Ingomar Vang.

witch it is mi dooti to you and your dad hoo was vary good too me and myne, as long as he had ennething too be good with, I want to tel yoo too kepe yoor wether-ey pield. wereas The Undersyned tels no lyes too no man, yoo kepe a sharp look out from yoor manemast and yoor fore-mast, fore yoo ma ·look out fore Skuawls. The Man's nam is Engström and he is a swed. i se him go to Prebensen evre da, and i se bi the skulkin' luk in his ey that he is the man fore Prebensen's durte jobs. So you luk out. This is rit bi yoor respekted and Devoted sarvent

TOBIAS TRULSON seccund
mat on board the bark *petrel.*

That these two letters, coming simultane-ously from two persons who had had no communication with each other, meant some-thing serious, Ingomar could not for a moment doubt. That his late visitor Lindgren was the same man as Engström and was a spy in Prebensen's employ, was more difficult to believe.

But it was easy to solve that riddle. The only thing Prebensen wanted was the bombs; and Ingomar knew exactly the number which he had in his possession. He stood for a while fumbling for the key in his pocket. His fingers felt numb and cold, while his face was burning hot. He had a foreboding of calamity, and scarcely dared to put the key into the key-hole.

But the operation was superfluous. He saw, in an instant, that the lock was broken. The discovery caused him no surprise. With trembling hands he grasped the box containing the bombs. There were three missing. A year ago this treachery on the part of one whom he had treated with kindness and courtesy would have saddened and discouraged Ingomar. Now it had the opposite effect. The fact that such extraordinary efforts were made to get possession of his secret proved to him how valuable it was.

He resolved to act promptly and not allow himself to be outwitted.

It was perfectly plain to him how and why the thing had happened. Mr. Prebensen had made the mistake of taking an engineer into his confidence, instead of a chemist; and the engineer, being unable to read the record of Ingomar's experiments, had come in person to procure specimens of the bombs for the purpose of having them analyzed.

As he was unable to analyze them himself, he would have to send them to a chemist. Thereby he would lose a few days; and by taking advantage of this, the rightful inventor hoped to defeat the dishonest scheme.

He lost no time in telegraphing an application for a patent and a full description of his invention to the patent-offices in Christiania and London; and when Sir Robert returned, the same evening, they started together for Hull, whence, the following morning, they took the steamer for Norway.

But here a surprise was in store for them. Lindgren was the first man they met on board the steamer. He had evidently thought it the safer course to employ an English chemist rather than a Norwegian one. He shook hands with Sir Robert and Ingomar, declared himself delighted to have the pleasure of their society during the voyage, and acted so much like an innocent man that Ingomar began to question himself whether he had not, after all, unjustly suspected him. If it had not been for the skulking look in the Swede's eye, he would have attributed the loss of the bombs to some mysterious accident.

Sir Robert, however, had seen too much of· the world to be led astray by the swindler's cordiality. When they arrived in Christiania, about eleven o'clock in the forenoon, he took no thought of his baggage, but grabbing his *protégé* by the arm jumped into the first cab he caught sight of, and told the cabman to drive as fast as he could to the Patent Office.

They had just turned the first corner of Custom House Street, when they saw Lindgren, who had secured a much better horse, dash past them.

"Look here!" cried Ingomar to the Jehu,
rising up in his cab; "if you can get us to
the Patent Office before that fellow in the
cab there, it is ten dollars in your pocket."

"Twenty!" shouted Sir Robert, holding
up his ten fingers under the impression that
he had twice that number; "twenty dollars
in your pocket!"

But, unhappily, the driver was one of those
slow-witted fellows whom it takes five minutes to comprehend any statement, however
simple. To the unutterable dismay of the
baronet, he stopped his horse, and with innocent stupidity inquired where the Patent
Office was. In the mean while Lindgren's
cab had disappeared around another corner.

"Why did n't you tell us before, you block-
head, that you did n't know it?" thundered
Sir Robert.

Jehu, not understanding English, asked
what he could do for the gentlemen. If the
honorable gentleman was ill, he knew where
to find a doctor.

"Oh, you sublime donkey!" yelled the
enraged baronet, "don't you comprehend

that every moment you waste is worth a fortune?"

Wasting no more words, Ingomar sprang up on the box, seized the reins, and whipped up the horse. But, unhappily, he had no more idea of where the Patent Office was than the driver, who, deprived of his dignity, began to swear and to yell, "Police!"

Two burly guardians of the peace came rushing up in response to his call, seized the horse by the bit, and could only with difficulty be dissuaded from arresting the travellers. Paying the driver twenty crowns in order to pacify him, Sir Robert and Ingomar jumped out of the cab, and inquiring the way of the policemen finally reached the Patent Office.

As they had expected, they found Lindgren's cab standing outside. With their hearts in their throats they darted up the long flight of stairs, and having entered the reception-room, found Lindgren in earnest conversation with one of the officials.

"But, my dear sir," they heard the official say, "that is the very patent that was applied for by telegraph, three days ago, by one Ingomar Vang."

"I didn't suppose an application by telegraph was legal," objected Lindgren, turning his head and glaring savagely at the man he was trying to defraud.

"When accompanied by descriptions and specifications, it is perfectly legal," the official replied.

"I protest!" exclaimed the Swede. "The invention is mine; it was stolen from me."

"If you are able to prove that, you can get the patent cancelled, and your application will be considered."

Sir Robert, who had listened with boundless amazement, could contain himself no longer.

"Look here, young man," he said, stepping forward and laying a heavy hand on the Swede's shoulder, "I charge you to your face and in the presence of these gentlemen, with theft. If you don't make yourself scarce, I'll have you in jail before night."

It was now Lindgren's turn to be amazed. His uneasy glance wandered about the room;

but he did not dare to meet Ingomar's or Sir Robert's eye.

"Excuse me, sir," he said, with embarrassment to the official, "I'll call again, later, when we are safe from interruptions."

If there had been no other evidence of his guilt, the way he darted out of the door would have been enough to prejudice any jury. Ingomar now produced his model, explained its working, and at the end of a month secured his patent.

CHAPTER VII.

VENGEANCE OVERTAKES THE CONSUL.

WHILE his steamboat was being built on the Clyde, Ingomar spent much of his time in superintending the details of the construction. He invented also an important improvement, which fascinated Sir Robert's fancy. This was a pair of iron wings, which could be folded like those of a bird, and again spread out under the water so as to act as a break, increasing the ship's power of resistance when the harpooned whale took it in tow.

I doubt if Aladdin, when his gorgeous palace rose out of the ground, was half as happy as the young Norseman when he saw his daring thought gradually take shape in steel and iron. He walked about in a joyous excitement, sang to himself, and shouted with delight.

He had no doubt now of the success of his plans. Full of confidence in the future, he named his steamer the " Phœnix."

It was his first purpose to name it " Sir Robert Graham," in honor of his benefactor, and to let it remain his property, while keeping for himself only his patent rights in the harpoon gun; but to this Sir Robert objected. He did not want to speculate in his friend's genius, he said. He would take a mortgage in the steamer for its entire value, but vest the ownership in Ingomar, who could then, in case of success, repay the amount at his leisure.

It was accordingly thus arranged, and the launching of the steamer was fixed for the tenth of April, Lady Graham's birthday. In the mean while Ingomar was to return to his native town, and engage a captain and crew.

The prospect of appearing in Vardöe clothed with such authority gave him a sense of importance which he keenly relished. At the age of eighteen to have reached the dignity of an employer was an achievement

which more than satisfied his ambition. He
determined to offer Tobias the position of
first mate. What eyes the honest fellow
would make when such promotion was
offered him! And then to throw off the
detested yoke of Prebensen, and re-enter the
service of the firm of Vang & Co., — that
would be joy indeed!

Ingomar spent the four or five days of the
voyage from Hull in making out the list of
the men he would engage, for he knew every
sailor in the town, and his reputation for skill
and sobriety. The only trouble was that
they were now all in Prebensen's employ,
and the consul would regard the effort to engage them as a declaration of war.

Nevertheless, as the war had to come
sooner or later, Ingomar resolved to take a
bold stand, and not to shrink from the fight.

He knew that his enemy was shrewd and
unscrupulous, and he was prepared for every
kind of shabby trick and underhand ma-
noeuvre; but he would have his eyes open,
and not allow himself to be caught napping.
He had seen something of the world now,

and had greater confidence in himself. He was neither friendless nor penniless, as he was two years ago, when Prebensen thought he could crush him, as he would an insect, under his heel.

It was about noon one day in the middle of March that Ingomar arrived in his native town. The voyage had been stormy, and would have been tedious if his own happy thoughts had not afforded him entertainment. The sky was yet a trifle overcast, but the sun was breaking through the clouds as the boat steamed up the Busse Sound.

It struck the young traveller as singular that beside the mail sloop in which old Mr. Vang was, not a single craft came out to meet the steamer. Ordinarily the harbor swarmed with yawls and wherries on steamer days, and half the population thronged down on the quays, some eager for news, others looking for a job, and many from mere curiosity; but to-day, in spite of the fair weather, the quays were deserted.

When the accommodation ladder was lowered, Ingomar ran down to greet his father, whose face, he noticed, wore a troubled and anxious look.

"What's the matter, father?" he cried. "Is there an epidemic in town?"

"No," Mr. Vang answered; "but there is a riot."

"A riot!"

"Yes, the garrison has been called out, but the soldiers have been obliged to return to the fortress. The people are terribly enraged."

"Against whom?"

"Against Prebensen."

"Prebensen! And what has he done?"

"Well, you know the fisheries failed outright this winter on account of the terrible weather. There has been great distress here, and several poor people have actually starved to death. Prebensen's sea-booths were bursting with provisions of all kinds; but he refused to sell except for cash, and as the people had no cash, he let them starve. Listen! Do you hear that?"

A piercing yell, indescribably wild and fierce, followed by a chorus of hoarse screams, came floating over the water, and in the same moment a column of smoke, dense and black, rose into the still air.

" They are firing the sea-booths!" exclaimed Mr. Vang, with a terrified countenance. " They may burn the whole town! That man, that man! I warned him long ago, but he sneered at me, and prated about business principles. Now vengeance will overtake him."

The mail-pouches had by this time been received from the steamer, and the prow of the sloop was pointed toward shore.

" It seems odd that the people did n't attack the sea-booths long before this, when they have been starving all winter," Ingomar remarked.

" You may indeed say so. What caused the outbreak to-day was the news that Prebensen's ' Walrus ' — an old ram-shackle concern that ought long ago to have been condemned — has been wrecked off the Hebrides, and all the crew perished. And it has leaked out, too, through a clerk in the bank, that the consul must have known of the wreck long ago, but has kept it secret; for he has had time to collect his insurance. Yesterday, it is said, he deposited the check of an English marine insurance company for fifty thousand crowns.[1] It was this rumor which started the riot. That was the straw that broke the camel's back."

"But who started the riot? Somebody must have taken the lead."

"Your old friend Tobias. He has a long score to settle with Prebensen. Besides, his brother Marcus was mate on the 'Walrus,' and was drowned with the rest."

The three oarsmen, who were visibly anxious to have a hand in the spoils, pulled for dear life; and as soon as the boat bumped against the wharf, they ran up the stairs and made for the scene of the conflagration. Mr. Vang and Ingomar were obliged to help the mail-clerk carry the letter-pouches up to the post-office.

"It is God's mercy that there is no wind to speak of," said Mr. Vang; "otherwise the fire might spread over the whole town."

[1] About ten thousand dollars.

" But a big fire is apt to produce a wind," his son replied. " It would be a pity if all the town were to suffer for Prebensen's villany."

The bells were now tolling the alarm from the church-tower, and two cannon-shots from the ramparts of the fortress made the doors shake and the windows rattle in the post-office building.

Father and son hurried through the empty streets, each with a dim fear that some awful calamity was at hand. The smoke came rolling like a black pall over the house-tops, and the smell of burning wood and tar filled the air.

The old-fashioned fire-engine with its un-wieldy hand-pump came lumbering, in a leisurely manner, down the hill, but seemed in no haste; and half-a-dozen citizens in the uniform of the volunteer fire company strolled along after it, carrying red-painted buckets of leather which they were by law required to have hanging under the ceiling in the en-trance to their court-yards.

It was easy to see that they did not regard the destruction of Consul Prebensen's sea-

booths as a personal disaster. Nor, to be
candid, did Ingomar take Prebensen's loss
much to heart. The only one of the family
for whom he had a kindly feeling was Ragna,
and he did not imagine that she would be
seriously affected by this fire.

But what made him uneasy was the fear
lest the fire, if left unchecked, might gain
such headway that with the poor and awk-
ward engines it would be impossible to extin-
guish it.

Filled with this dread, he stopped at his
home only long enough to fling his valise on
a chair and kiss his sister, who had for a
week looked forward to his arrival in happy
excitement.

The church bells were still tolling with a
deep, tremulous apprehension, as he bounded
down the front stairs and rushed toward the
wharves. Rude noise and laughter, wild yells
and shouts, and occasional hoarse cheers
reached his ears, and gave him an idea of
what was going on before he reached the
scene. The red flames were now leaping
toward the sky, obscured for the moment by

a cloud of dense brown smoke, from which again they burst forth with wilder vehemence, accompanied by a dull, steady roar like the draught of a tremendous furnace.

Now and then a brilliant shower of sparks rushed upward with a loud crackle as some new, inflammable stuff caught fire.

Two large sea-booths, both belonging to Prebensen, were burning, and a third was threatened. Enormous quantities of goods were piled along the sides of the streets; barrels of molasses and sugar, bags of coffee, boxes of tea, hams, salted beef, smoked sausages, and bales of yarn and cloth were tumbled helter-skelter in the gutters and on the sidewalks.

The strong smell of rum which pervaded the air explained to Ingomar much that had happened. Three big hogsheads had been knocked open, and everybody was helping himself to his heart's desire. The pavement for half a dozen squares showed tracks of sugar and flour and salt, and pungent spices made people sneeze who had torn open the bags in the hope of finding something eatable.

About the burning sea-booths the streets were packed with excited men and women, who cursed and yelled, swaying hither and thither, some trying to get away with bags of stolen provisions, others guying them and tearing the booty from their hands. Some were intoxicated, but the majority were more intent upon satisfying their vengeance than their thirst.

When Ingomar had reached the outskirts of the crowd, he found them rushing with angry screams and gestures against the two old fire-engines, which they were determined to prevent from putting out the fire.

"Go it, boys, go it!" shouted a voice, which he recognized as that of Tobias. "Let the old bloodhound get his due! We don't want no engines. Keep 'em away, mates! That's right! Break the handles! Cut the ropes! Let her hum, — the old ramshackle! Don't have no mercy on Pre-bensen! There was many a brave lad aboard the 'Walrus,' but he hadn't no mercy on them."

Tobias had climbed up on a pile of bales

and boxes in order to make himself heard,
and his stalwart form and coppery face stood
out in strong relief against the burning sea-
booths.

Every sentence he uttered was greeted
with cheers; and before he had finished, the
crowd rushed against the fire-corps that had
charge of the engines and drove them back.
They were just about to demolish the de-
crepit machine when Ingomar sprang forward, mounted the pump, and cried, —

"Stand back, lads! If you don't want to
burn the town, you've got to put out this
fire!"

His sudden appearance there, when he was
supposed to be a thousand miles away, had
an almost magical effect. He was well liked
by all; and the story of his achievements in
England, which had been immensely exaggerated, had made them proud of him
as well.

"Why, Ingomar!" "That's Ingomar!"
half-a-dozen voices ejaculated. "Get down,
Ingomar! Surely you are the last one to
take that bloodhound Prebensen's part!" an

old pilot added, nodding with friendly familiarity to the young man.

"No, lads, I don't take Prebensen's part," Ingomar replied, in so loud a voice that he could be heard by all. "I am with you, heart and soul, as against Prebensen. But what harm are you doing Prebensen by burning up his sea-booths, which are insured for all they are worth and probably more? You don't want to burn up the town surely; and that is what you will be doing, if you don't allow the fire company to get near enough to protect the nearest buildings."

"He is right!" the soberer among the throng exclaimed; "he's right! Let the engines pass!"

Leaping down, Ingomar with a dozen others took hold of the foremost engine, and dragged it down in front of the burning seabooths. The crowd opened a path for him; and the other engine soon followed. Quickly he formed the men into lines, reaching from the wharf into the street; and the red leather buckets were handed up, filled, by the one line, and returned empty by the other.

He was congratulating himself that everything was going smoothly, when he saw Tobias break ruthlessly through the lines and advance toward him.

"Who is boss here, I should like to know," asked the mate, angrily, — "you or I ?"

" The one who can make himself obeyed," answered Ingomar.

" Look here, lad," Tobias continued, suddenly cooling down, " I don't want to fight you. But you must n't come and meddle here. To-day I mean to settle my score with Prebensen, if it is to be the last day of my life. Stand back, lad, and let 's be friends ! "

" You stand back yourself, Tobias ! " retorted Ingomar, firmly. " You can't burn the town because you have a grudge against Prebensen. When I have put out this fire, I 'll talk with you all you like, but now I have not the time."

He formed his lines again, and soon had four columns of water playing upon the fire. His eyes were everywhere; his ringing tones of command were heard above all the noise.

Seeing that one of the neighboring booths was in danger, he had wet sails brought from the ships in the harbor, and hanging these over the exposed walls and roofs saved them from catching fire from the flying sparks. He was so absorbed in these various tasks that he did not observe what was going on on the outskirts of the crowd. There Tobias had gathered an excited group about him, — most of them relatives of the lost crew of the "Walrus," — and was addressing them in this fashion : —

" It is true, as the lad says. We 've made him richer and not poorer by burning his sea-booths, just as the storm made him richer by foundering the 'Walrus.' His skinny old carcass, — that 's the only thing of his which we can hurt, — and that no insurance company can patch for him. Let 's make him smart, mates, for the ill he has done us."

With about thirty furious men he started in the direction of Prebensen's mansion ; but before they had reached the middle of the next block, their number was more than doubled. It soon became rumored

where they were going; and a great multitude, to whom the fire could afford no more
entertainment, set themselves in motion and
rushed up the street toward the consul's
residence.

At the time when Tobias was addressing
the crowd, Prebensen was sitting quietly in
his office, talking with the chief of police.

"Just watch them carefully," he was saying; "take down the names of the ring-
leaders and every one who carries anything
off. Before another month we shall have
them in jail, with stand-up collars about their
necks, every mother's son of them!"

"Exactly, Mr. Consul, exactly!" answered
the chief of police, rubbing his hands de-
lightedly. "I'll take care to collect all the
testimony which we may require."

"That's business!" cried the consul, with
a dry, mirthless laugh; "in jail, every one of
them, — six, nine, and twelve years, — that'll
teach them respect for capital, eh, Mr.
Chief?"

The chief of police rose and took his leave.
Prebensen followed him to the door, bowing.

He had just turned his back on the exalted official, when a subdued roar, like that of a cataract, fell upon his ears. He faced about toward the street again, and saw in the distance the furious mob approaching. He grew suddenly as pale as a ghost.

"Hansen! Jensen! Olsen!" he cried to the clerks; "bar the doors! Put up the iron shutters, quick! For God's sake, hurry!"

Swift as an arrow, he darted toward the money-drawer, which he pulled out, and rushed into the inner office, the door of which he closed behind him. The most conspicuous object there was a great safe, like that of a bank, which was built into the wall, displaying the backs of ledgers and metal boxes filled with money and securities.

Emptying the contents of the money-drawer, with nervous haste, into a linen bag, and quickly collecting all papers of value on the desk, the consul, casting a terrified glance toward the windows, which the clerks were darkening with the huge shutters, unlocked the two heavily bolted doors of the safe and stepped into the vault.

At that very moment his son Sophus, who had discovered the mob from an upper window, came rushing into the room to give warning; and seeing the dusky interior and the door of the safe open, he supposed his father, in his fright, had left the room, forgetting to lock it.

Flinging himself against the huge door with his whole weight, he slammed it, and beside himself with fear, yelled to the clerks to arm themselves with pistols and harpoons or anything they could lay hold of.

He did not hear the smothered shriek from within the safe; for he was already half-way up the stairs, carrying an old rifle with a bayonet, which the clerk Hansen had handed him.

Prebensen had purposely had his safe so made that it could be hastily locked, without the use of the elaborate combination. The inner bolts were supplied with springs, and the ends so rounded on one side that they would catch like the latch of a door. Suspicious as he was, he had always been afraid that any one should discover how rich he was, and it had therefore always been his custom quickly to slam the door of the safe before admitting any one to the office.

Now he stood within this narrow vault, numb with terror, pulling desperately at the heavy steel bars, which mocked his feeble exertions.

The wealth he had labored for since his earliest years — for the sake of which he had sacrificed friendship, gratitude, and affection, nay, his very soul — was round about him.

Bags heavy with gold and silver coin, drawers full of precious securities, — English consols, United States bonds, Prussian funds, — all that was safest and best in the world of finance, — all these things, for which he had hungered, and for the sake of which he had loaded his name with curses, were within the grasp of his hand; but, alas! how worthless they were to him now! A breath of vital air — the cheapest and commonest boon, which even the poorest mortal possesses in abundance — would be a thousand times more precious than all the hoarded wealth of the Indies.

Hush! What is that? Strange, hollow noises resound through the house, — dull thuds, as of heavy things falling; quick explosions, as of pistol-shots, and then an angry, surging roar like that of the ocean breaking over an embankment.

The consul with a wild despair grabs the steel bars of the door, and pulls and wrenches and tugs at them; but it is all in vain. A white mist swims about him; his blood throbs and hammers in his temples; faint, red flames dance before his eyes; an oppressive weariness steals over him; his limbs feel as heavy as lead.

Once, twice, thrice he tries to raise his voice and shriek, but not a sound can he produce. Again, wild, faint noises, through which pierce keen cries of terror. Yes; he knows now what it means. His house is being plundered by the mob; his wife and children are, perhaps, being maltreated for his sake. So this is to be the end of all his ceaseless toil and ambition! He remembered suddenly Vang's warning words, "They are now at your mercy, but the day

may come when you will **be at their mercy."**
That day had come.

He wished now he **had** heeded Vang's
warning. **He** might have been **a** blessing **to**
the **community in** which he lived, without
greatly diminishing his wealth. He might
have **reaped benedictions** instead of curses.
As he thought of this, an impatient regret,
which cut like a sharp sword, pierced his
heart.

But his faintness grew upon him, and out
of it he glided **gradually** into the deeper
unconsciousness of the long, long night.

Tobias, at the head of the angry mob,
was pounding with a sledge-hammer at **the**
front door of Prebensen's **mansion.** He had
shouted **repeatedly to the clerks to** open, but
they were as yet more afraid of the consul
than they were of him. Bareheaded, with
torn clothes and a blackened face purple
with rage, the mate tried to batter down the
door, swearing **and** shouting between **each**
blow of the huge hammer.

The upper panel suddenly split, and **in**
two minutes the whole **door was** broken into

splinters. Tobias burst into the house with his sledge raised above his head, and the crowd followed after him.

"Where is Prebensen?" they yelled. "Let's find Prebensen!"

They first spread through the store and the other rooms of the first floor, and helped themselves to what they could find, but not a trace of Prebensen could they discover. Next the cellar was. ransacked, and every closet searched, but the consul was and remained invisible.

They had wrought themselves into such a frenzy of indignation at the thought of his escaping, that no plan of vengeance seemed now too violent. Under Tobias's lead they stormed up to the second floor, and there they met with the first obstacle to their progress.

At the head of the stairs stood a tall young girl of sixteen, with a pale, determined face. In her hand she held the old unloaded rifle with a bayonet at the end.

"Stand back!" she cried; "the first one who tries to pass is a dead man."

A chorus of jeers from the mob greeted this challenge.

Tobias, judging from the bayonet that the rifle was not loaded, raised his sledge and was about to knock it out of her hands, when some one broke wildly through the crowd and shouted, " Don't dare to touch her ! "

In the next moment Ingomar had wrested the hammer out of the mate's grasp, and lifted it threateningly over his head.

" Fall back ! " he commanded. " Who of you is such a coward as to molest a lady ? "

"We want Prebensen ! We want Preben-sen ! " yelled a hundred voices.

"I beg of you, friends, to leave this house, and not disgrace yourselves by further violence."

He stood now at Ragna's side, barring the way, so that no one could pass. He was confident, too, that no one would attack him, and Tobias least of all.

Within an hour the crowd had dispersed, and the Prebensen mansion was saved.

CHAPTER VIII.

IT was a bright sunny day about the middle of April, three weeks after Consul Prebensen's funeral. All the wharves were black with people; every boat was loaded to the water's edge, and on the spars and masts of the ships in the harbor small boys and sailors crawled, like flies under the ceiling.

The sky was a vast shining vault, the water glittered in the sun like a burnished shield, and the downy brood of auks and eider-ducks that swam upon its surface in tranquil companies of twenty or a hundred, looked as if they found swimming a delightful occupation.

The black profile of the Horn Island traced its jagged outline against the horizon, but its myriad noisy colonists had suspended their quarrels for the moment, for they, too, seemed to have a notion that something extraordinary was going on in their immediate neighborhood.

What they saw was a small black steamboat, with red funnels and a gilded figurehead representing the bird Phœnix rising, with outspread wings, from its ashes; and above the figure-head was mounted a gilded swivel-gun which shot long, dazzling beams in the sunshine.

To judge by its motions, this small steamer had surely gone mad. Now it darted forward at the top of its speed; now it suddenly flung itself about, pressing on with tremendous force, while the spray flew about its prow, and the long foaming swell in its wake rocked thousands of rainbow-tinted bubbles and pushed shoreward a procession of shining billows.

There was an air of relentless energy and dogged determination in the little black monster which made the sailors in the mast-tops confident that whatever it had set out to do it would be sure to accomplish; but the staid old citizens on the wharf, as they watched its strange manœuvres through their telescopes, shook their heads, and asked one another what the world was coming to.

"'Phœnix,'" observed the chief of police to the commander on the fortress, as he read the name, — "was n't he a king some- wheres?"

"Yes," answered the commander, "he was the fellow who said that you should call no man happy until he was dead."

"Pretty level-headed chap, that same old Phœnix!" the chief remarked.

But look! Now this same "Phœnix" seems anything but level-headed. She is heading right for the shore. She will surely run aground. On a little platform in the foremast Tobias is seen signalling to the captain. Suddenly the boat swings vio- lently to starboard, so that her beams creak and her knees groan in their fastenings. A mighty column of water shoots into the air not fifty feet from the bow.

"Fire!" screams Ingomar's voice from the bridge. A red flash, an ear-splitting bang!

The barbed harpoon darts forth, and is buried deep in the belly of the whale. Now let go the line! The enormous bluish-black bulk is seen shooting through the clear waves, with the harpoon in its side dragging the heavy line after it.

It is an exciting sight. Far, far down into the cool pale-green deep you can follow the huge beast, and see its elephantine efforts to rid itself of the troublesome iron claw that sticks in its flesh. It flings itself about from one side to the other; it changes its course abruptly; it shakes its monstrous tail, it opens and shuts its cavernous gap in wrathful impatience.

But soon the fifteen minutes, during which the air in its lungs will suffice, have expired. It is forced to rise again to draw a fresh breath.

Up it comes, — up through the transparent emerald sea; its motions are sluggish, and a long crimson trail spreads from its wounded side. A blue-black island, like a submarine rock, is slowly raised to the surface of the water; a column of spray is blown into the air, and again the animal dives, painfully, ponderously, with laborious difficulty.

Soon the entire length of the line is run out. The whale gives a pull, and a mighty one; then calmly continues its course, taking the "Phœnix" in tow. The captain reverses the engines, but the twenty-horse power is as nothing against the strength of the great leviathan.

Foaming, shrieking, perspiring, churning the water excitedly with its toiling screw, the "Phœnix" is dragged out toward the open sea. Ingomar and Sir Robert, who stand on the bridge, exchange anxious glances.

"Now steady, my boy! We are not at the end of the game yet," the baronet observes encouragingly, putting his hand on Ingomar's shoulder.

"I know the bomb has exploded!" the latter exclaims; "but it won't kill at once."

"I did n't hear anything."

"You can't hear anything, except, perhaps, a dull thud within the body of the whale."

For half an hour the steamer, fighting des-

perately like a naughty child, pursued its reluctant way toward the Arctic wilderness.

"Now, Captain, let us try our wings!"
cried Ingomar.

Instantly a gigantic pair of steel wings,
shaped like those of a butterfly, is spread
out. The whale pulls again, and the "Phœnix" trembles from bow to stern. Ingomar
trembles too, as he stands clutching the rail-
ing of the bridge, and gazes with a troubled
look at the placid ocean. He knows that
this is the critical moment.

Has the bomb exploded, or has it not?
His heart throbs with a suffocating speed,
then seems to stop. One minute passes,
and an intolerably long one! Then, as the
"Phœnix" shoots forward at half speed, —
as if afraid of what it will discover, — a dark,
gigantic mass is seen slowly, slowly rising
into view. And this time no water is blown
into the air. The whale is dead!

A cry of relief escapes the anxious inventor. It was as if life and death trembled in
the balance. He draws a long breath from
the bottom of his lungs.

"The whale floats!" he cries, in a delirium of joy. "It floats, Sir Robert! it floats!"

Cheer upon cheer rends the air! Every sailor on board swings his cap, and yells with all the might of his lungs. Sir Robert grabs the young man's hand, and wrings it as if he would wring it off, and gazes at his radiant face with eyes in which tears of joy glitter.

"My dear boy," he cries, as soon as he has found his voice, "you have won the battle, though you fought against heavy odds!"

Ingomar stares back at Sir Robert and tries to speak; but there is a lump in his throat, and for a while he cannot utter a word.

"Sir Robert," he manages at last to stammer, "it was *we* who fought the battle; it was *we* who won the victory, — for without you I should never have seen this day."

The chase was at an end.

The whale was taken in tow; and slowly and cautiously the "Phœnix" began her return voyage. It was valuable booty she

THE INVENTION IS SUCCESSFUL.

had secured this time! It was the future
of the town of Vardöe, nay, of all Finmark, which she dragged after her at the
rate of three knots an hour. For if the whale
could be towed ashore, then all the parts of
its enormous carcass, which on the ocean
must be wasted, could be utilized. The flesh
and bones could be made into fertilizers
which would enrich the poor soil of Finmark
and make it profitable to cultivate; the blubber could be boiled and the oil refined with
modern machinery; much could be saved in
freight and in wages of crew, when the voyage was shortened to as many days as it
formerly took months.

Ingomar, as he stood on the bridge, steaming in his own vessel back to the city of his
birth, saw his future unfold itself before him
in daring visions. With this ship "Phœnix,"
not only his own family's fortunes, but the
fortunes of the town, should rise from their
ashes. Justice and generosity — the law of
the Golden Rule — should be his motto.

Prebensen's yoke of cruel and narrow self-
interest, which in the end defeats itself,

should no more oppress the people and
keep them in abject poverty. The house
of Vang & Son, reinstated in its old position of prosperity and eminence, would
undo the wrong that Prebensen had done,
and reap blessings where the latter had
reaped curses.

These were the young man's thoughts as
he sailed up the Busse Sound, followed by
screaming swarms of sea-birds, who by their
multitude almost obscured the daylight. For
a dead whale means a feast to gulls and auks
and cormorants; and they are not bashful in
claiming their share of the booty. Then,
too, the people on shore knew what this
winged host meant; they shouted themselves hoarse, and swung hats, caps, and
handkerchiefs. Long, gayly colored stream-
ers adorned the ships on the harbor; flags
were run up on many houses in town; guns
and cannon were fired on the wharves and
responded to by the " Phœnix."

Never had the town of Vardöe, since the
day of its foundation, seen such joyous commotion as it witnessed on this day. People

embraced one another in the streets from excess of happiness. And when Ingomar and Sir Robert stepped ashore, they were greeted with cheers, speeches, poems, and songs.

Ingomar was lifted bodily on the shoulders of the crowd and carried in triumph to his father's house.

There a little incident occurred which may be worth recording. In the hall, just as he entered, he saw a young lady, dressed in mourning, apparently waiting for him. As she threw her long black veil aside, he recognized **Ragna** Prebensen.

He knew all the painful circumstances connected with her father's death, and the finding of his body in the safe, and he respected her grief too much to be willing to flaunt his own happiness in her face.

But in her other feelings were uppermost. Without hesitation or embarrassment she advanced toward him, grasped his hand cordially, and said, —

"I could n't bear to be absent on the day of your triumph, Ingomar. You know you

told me, two years ago, that you were going
to be a great man, and I believed you then
and always. I want to congratulate you
with all my heart."

"I thank you, Ragna," he answered, a
little tremulously, for her generosity touched
him; "it is very kind of you to rejoice in my
good fortune. And my only regret is that
it seems to have been purchased at the
expense of your sorrow."

"Well, it cannot be otherwise," she murmured. "Your star is rising, ours has set;
and I am more glad on your account than
sad on my own."

She turned to go away, but he still held
her hand in his, as if reluctant to let her
leave him. "Ragna," he said warmly,
"your star has not set. Your star and mine
must rise together."

When at last the public celebration was
at an end, — though the small boys in the
street continued it until midnight, — Sir
Robert invited the government officials and
other prominent citizens to a magnificent
dinner on board the "Phœnix;" and it is

only out of regard for Ingomar's modesty that I refrain from repeating what was said in the speeches which were made at this banquet.

Let me only tell you this, that old Mr. Vang was so overcome with joy that he wept.

Exaggerated though they might seem, the prophecies that were made about Ingomar have not been falsified by his subsequent life. He had fought against heavy odds; but his indomitable pluck and perseverance had in the end triumphed. The value of his invention is now everywhere recognized; he has patented it in England, Germany, Holland, and France, and it has made him a rich man.

Vang & Son are now the greatest ship-owners in northern Norway, and the whole whaling industry is practically in their hands.

Mrs. Ingomar Vang, *née* Prebensen, seconds her husband heartily in his efforts to inspire the people with self-respect, and teach them cleanliness, sobriety, and regard for health

in their modes of living and in bringing up
their children. She has poverty, ignorance,
and often vice and inherited customs to fight
against; but she fights with a brave heart,
knowing that she has the support of her
noble and generous Ingomar. And this
thought, also, strengthens her purpose amid
many discouragements, — that she owes it to
this community which her father plundered,
to compensate with good deeds for all the
ill that he accomplished. Like a ministering
angel she goes from house to house, cheer-
ing, comforting, teaching, alleviating suffer-
ing, and wisely dispensing charity.

Ingomar is her hero now, as he always
was; and not only to her is he a hero, but to
the whole seafaring population of Norway.
Every Norse sailor regards it as an honor to
sail in his ships ; not only because he knows
that every ship that bears the name of Vang
& Son is sound in every joint, but because
the greatness to which the young owner has
risen from small beginnings dignifies every
man in his employ, and inspires him to labor
and to hope with a sturdy heart.

It is scarcely necessary to add that the qualities which made Ingomar's boyhood remarkable have not deserted him in his manhood. He has been and is yet a blessing to his native town, nay, to his native country.

THE END.